11/15

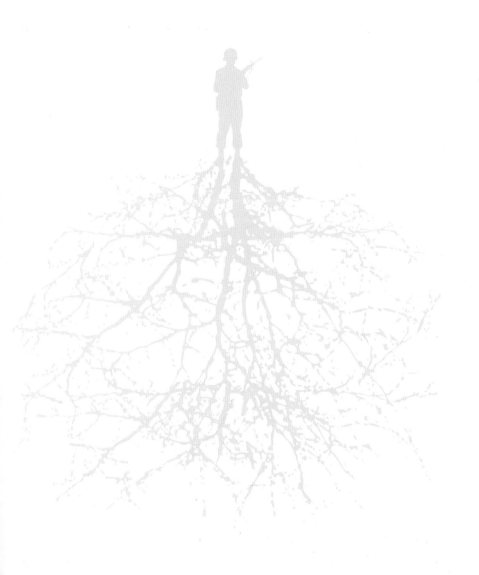

√

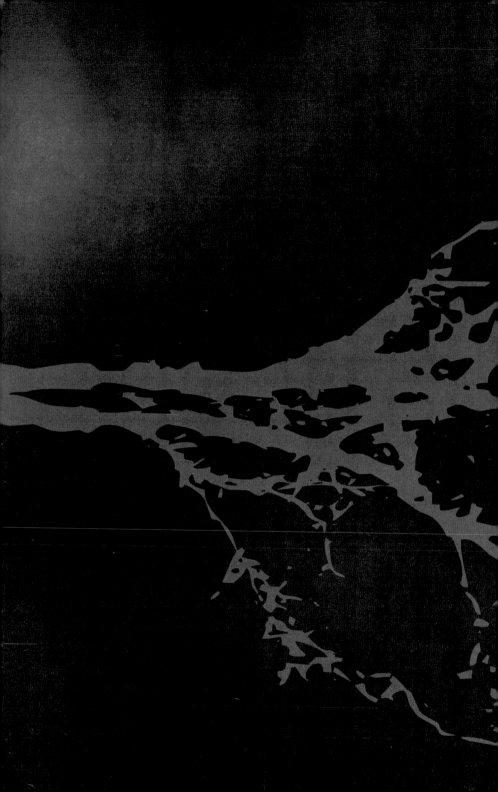

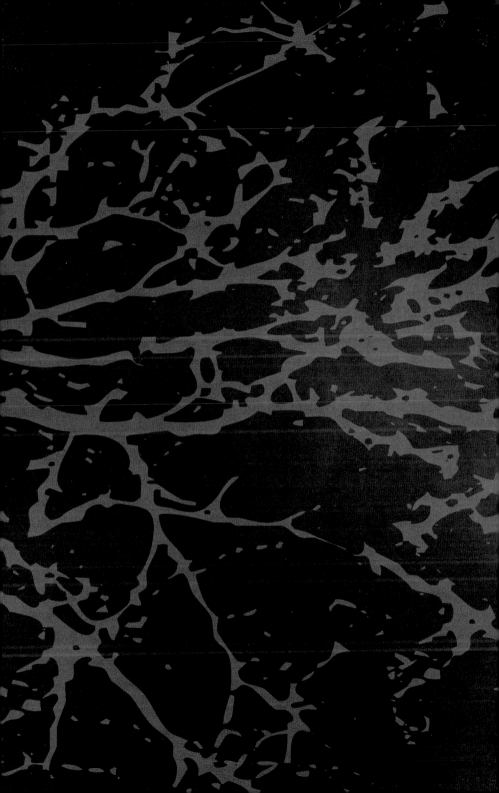

BLOODLINES
DAMAGE CONTROL

written by
M. Zachary Sherman

illustrated by
Josef Cage

colored by
Marlong Iligan

STONE ARCH BOOKS
a capstone imprint

DEDICATED TO THE MEN AND WOMEN
OF THE ARMED SERVICES

Bloodlines is published by Stone Arch Books,
A Capstone Imprint, 1710 Roe Crest Drive
North Mankato, MN 56003
www.capstonepub.com

Cataloging-in-Publication Data is available on
the Library of Congress website.
ISBN: 978-1-4342-3765-1 (library binding)
ISBN: 978-1-4342-3875-7 (paperback)

Summary: During the Korean War, a U.S. Army
cargo plane crashes behind enemy lines, and
soldiers of the 249th Engineer Battalion are
stranded. Facing a brutal environment and
attacks by enemy forces, Private First Class
Tony Donovan takes action! With spare parts
and ingenuity, he plans to repair a vehicle from
the wreckage and transport his comrades to
safety.

Art Director: Bob Lentz
Graphic Designer: Brann Garvey
Production Specialist: Michelle Biedscheid

Photo credits: Corel, 61; Getty Images Inc.: AFP/
STR, 34, Archive Photos/Bachrach, 35 (bottom),
Central Press, 75, Picture Post/Bert Hardy,
35 (top), Three Lions, 7, Time Life Pictures/
National Archives,18, Time Life Pictures/
National Archives/Frank C. Kerr, 47; M. Zachary
Sherman, 82, back cover; Shutterstock: Olivier
Le Queinec, 60; U.S. Marine Corps photo by
Corporal Peter McDonald, 46, Cpl. W.T. Wolfe, 74

Printed in the United States of America
in Stevens Point, Wisconsin.
122012   007083R

TABLE OF CONTENTS

PERSONNEL FILE

Private First Class
Tony Donovan

ORGANIZATION:
U.S. Army, 249th Engineer Battalion

ENTERED SERVICE AT:
Camp Pendleton, CA

BORN:
May 15, 1930

EQUIPMENT

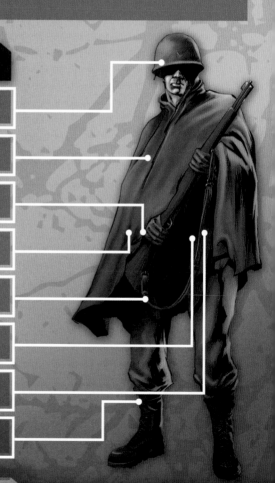

M1951 Winter Helmet

Military Poncho

M1951 Pistol Belt

Ammunition

M2 Garand

First-Aid Pouch

.45 Caliber Pistol

Combat Boots

OVERVIEW: KOREAN WAR

For thousands of years, people have fought over Korea. From 1910 until the end of World War II, Japan controlled the entire peninsula. However, after the war, Korea was divided into two parts. Russia controlled the northern half of the peninsula, and the United States controlled the southern half. Three years later, the two halves became independent nations — North Korea and South Korea. But their troubles were just beginning. On June 25, 1950, North Korea, led by their communist ruler Kim Il Sung, attacked the South. This action started what would become the Korean War.

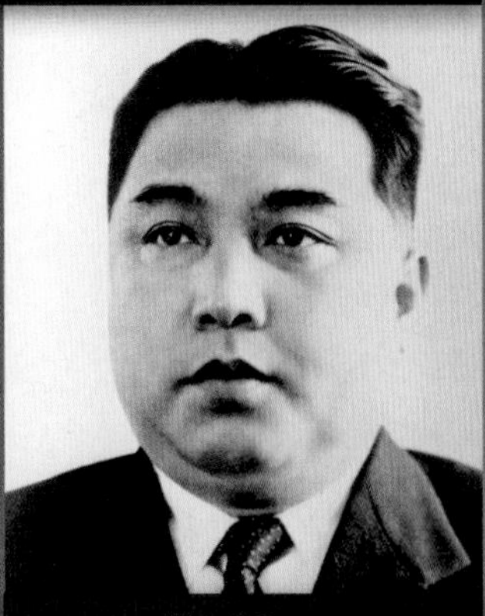

Kim Il Sung

MAP

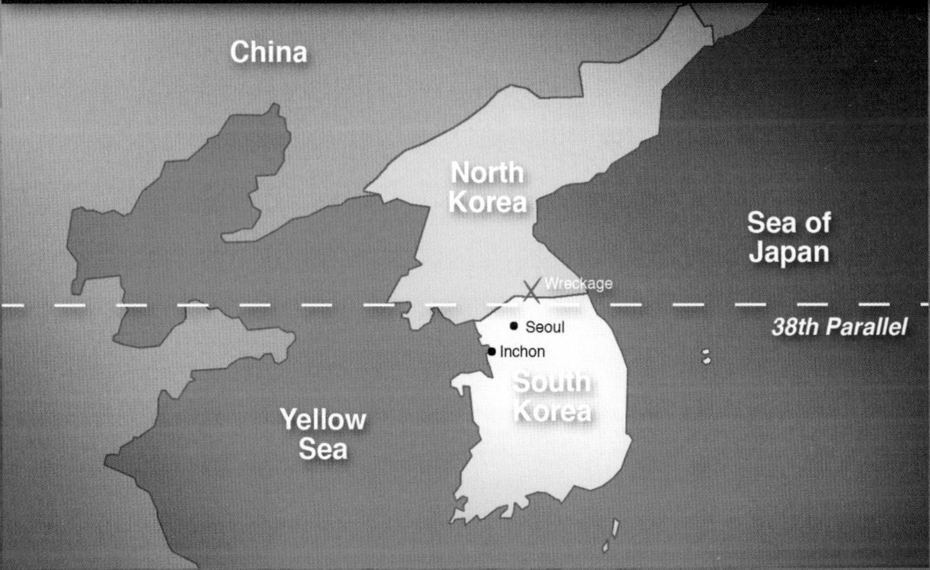
China
North Korea
Sea of Japan
Wreckage
38th Parallel
Seoul
Inchon
South Korea
Yellow Sea

MISSION

When a U.S. Army cargo plane crashes behind enemy lines, soldiers must repair a vehicle from the wreckage and evacuate to safety.

CHAPTER 001

SURVIVAL

"Richards? Donovan? Anyone?!"

The words echoed through the cabin of a mangled C-119 cargo plane, but they seemed to get swallowed up by choking flames. Twenty-four-year-old 2nd Lieutenant Drew Polaski stumbled around the interior of the downed aircraft. He coughed and waved thick smoke from his face. He squinted through the toxic black clouds, searching for his crew.

The main fuselage of the plane was tipped on its side. Sunlight streaked in from the gouges in its metal hull, life-taking wounds in the belly of the aircraft.

The battalion had crashed behind enemy lines — fifty kilometers from the Demilitarized Zone in the mountains of South Korea. It was a miracle anyone was alive. The pilot and copilot were gone, but they'd done their jobs. They'd landed the limping plane the best they could.

As the C-119 dropped from the skies, the ten men of 249th Engineer Battalion had braced for impact. But when the plane dipped, the chains strapping down their cargo had snapped like twine. The twin Woody jeeps, five pallets of supplies, and various engineering equipment had danced wildly around the cabin. So had the men. The soldiers were tossed around the plane like out-of-control ping-pong balls.

That is, until the plane had slammed into the side of a mountain. The entire front end of the aircraft had collapsed in like an accordion. Several of the soldiers hadn't survive the tremendous impact. The bodies of the dead were now scattered throughout the cargo bay.

Lieutenant Polaski continued searching through the wreckage for any signs of life. "Richards? Donovan?" he hollered again. This time, however, the sound of stirring metal caught his attention.

"I'm — I'm okay, sir," came a voice from under the spare hood of a jeep. It was Private First Class Tony Donovan. Slowly, the soldier pushed the hood aside and stood. He wiped debris off his green coverall uniform.

"You're bleeding," noted Polaski.

A trickle of crimson blood ran down Donovan's forehead. "I'm okay, sir," said the private. "But thanks." He quickly wiped the wound clean with his hand and smeared the blood on his trousers.

Private Donovan looked at the carnage around the plane. "How many, sir?" he asked his lieutenant.

Polaski bowed his head. "You're the first person I've found alive —" he began.

"But not the last!" called a voice from outside the cargo bay. "Out here!"

Donovan and Polaski rushed toward the shout. The tail section of the plane had been sheared clean off. In the middle of the wreckage, they spotted the massive silhouette of a man, slumped to his knees.

"Sarge!" Donovan called out, scrambling toward him.

Standing with Sergeant Richards were three other soldiers: Corporal DeLori, Corporal Reed, and Corporal Soares. They all looked worse for wear, but they were alive. That's all that mattered now.

"You okay, boys?" asked Lieutenant Polaski, following Donovan toward his troops.

"Not bad, considering the situation," answered Corporal Reed. He was still chewing one of his trademark sticks of Beeman's gum.

"How you doing, kid?" Sergeant Richards asked Donovan.

Donovan was shaken, but he didn't want to show it. "Well," replied Donovan, "any landing you can walk away from is a good one, right, Sarge?"

"Ha!" Richards laughed. "The kid's got a sense of humor, boys. Now I know I'm dead!"

The other men chuckled. But Donovan could tell right away that Lieutenant Polaski didn't see any humor in their situation. Jeep parts, tires, weapons, ammunition, and broken cases of rations littered the area.

"First order of business," the lieutenant said, "is setting up a perimeter — nothing, nobody gets through. DeLori, you take Corporal Soares and recon out twenty meters. Make sure we're alone in this jungle."

Corporal Reed and Soares glanced at one another.

"Yes, sir," DeLori finally mumbled. He looked back at the lieutenant with concern. "But —"

"But what, Corporal?" Polaski asked.

"We don't have any weapons, sir," replied DeLori. "What if we run into enemy patrols?"

Polaski cursed himself. "Hadn't thought of that, Corporal," he mumbled.

"Sir? If I may," Richards began.

The lieutenant glanced over. "Go ahead, Corporal," he said.

"One of the cargo crates had weapons and ammo inside," added Richards. "DeLori, Reed, and Soares, spread out and find it. Distribute one rifle and three magazines to each man. Give the lieutenant a sidearm if you find one. Understood?"

"Yes, Sergeant," said the other men. The corporals quickly spread out, clambering through the wreckage to find any precious cargo.

"Don't worry, sir," Richards told the lieutenant. "They'll find it. But what's the plan after they do?"

"We wait," replied Lieutenant Polaski.

"For what, sir?" asked Sergeant Richards.

"Rescue," said the lieutenant. "The pilot radioed our position as we went down. It's standard operating procedure — wait at the crash site until help arrives."

"No offense, sir," Richards began, "but the Korean Army's got this area locked down pretty tight. If we just wait here — with no operational radio — the rescue choppers might not spot us in time."

"Those are my orders, Sergeant!" Polaski snapped. "We wait for rescue! Got it?"

Richards clammed up tight. Private Donovan knew the sergeant wasn't happy to be shut down in front of an underling.

Fortunately, Donovan knew Richards was right. It was dangerous to remain out here — even *with* weapons. The local Korean Army patrols would come searching for survivors. Richards knew that, and so did Donovan.

Standing nearby, Donovan piped up nervously, hoping to break some of the tension between his two superiors. "It's gonna get dark soon, sir," he said. "I'd like to volunteer to schedule out a fire-watch rotation."

"Donovan's right," said Richards. "It's a good bet the enemy knows we're here. We should be on alert."

Lieutenant Polaski looked at the sergeant and nodded. "Get to it," he commanded. Then he turned and stumbled off toward the fallen aircraft's cockpit.

With the lieutenant out of earshot, Sergeant Richards shook his head. "This isn't good," he mumbled.

"What, Sarge?" Donovan asked, overhearing.

"The KPA's gonna be on us like a swarm of bees," Richards replied with a sigh. "That's the problem with new LTs. They wanna to do everything by the book, but they ain't got no common sense!"

Donovan chuckled and then looked at the horizon. The sun dipped behind the trees in the distance, casting a golden glow over the pitted aluminum hull of the downed aircraft.

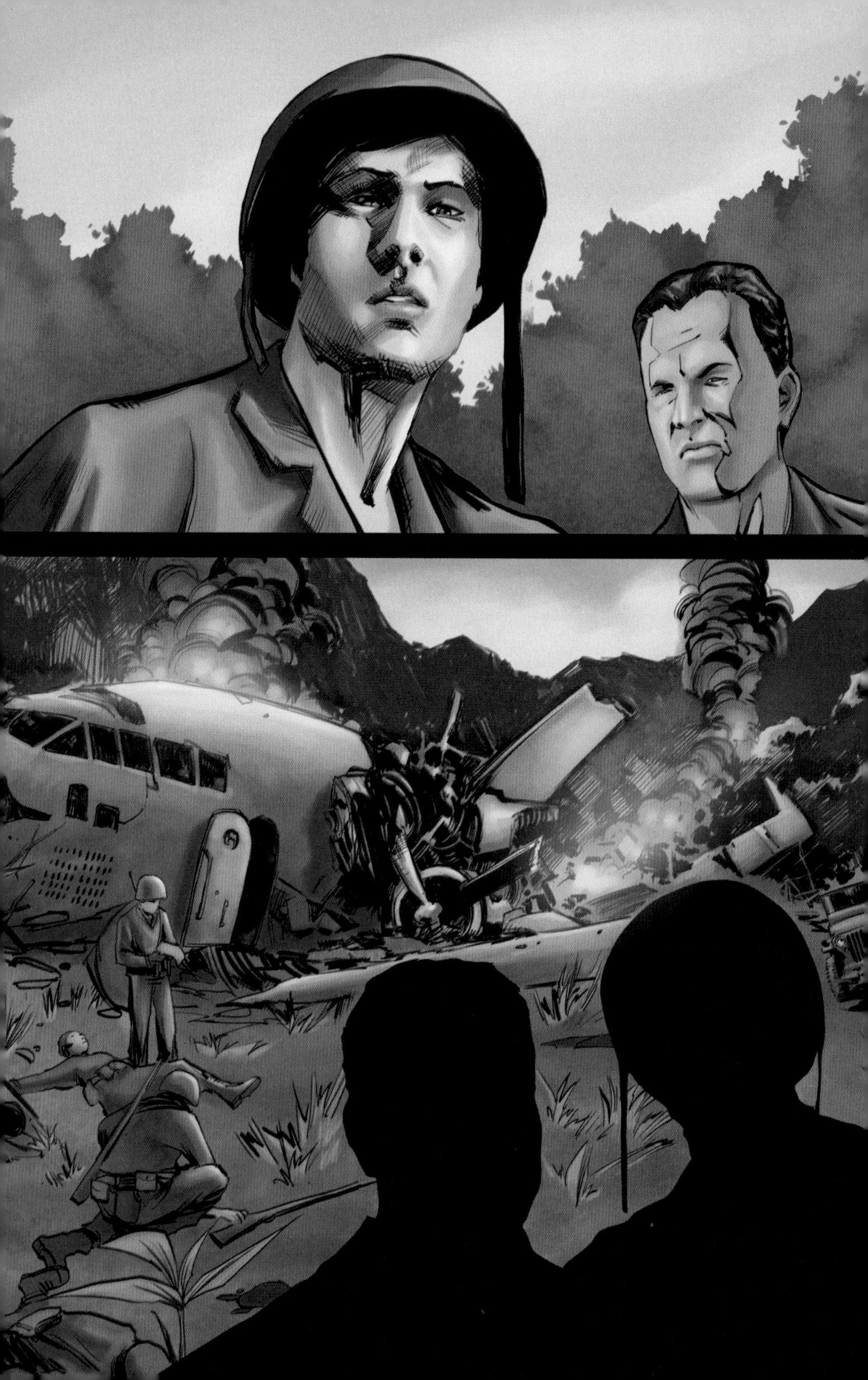

"It's going to be a long night," said Sergeant Richards. "Get that fire-watch rotation set. Schedule two-hour rotations between each man, and don't take the first watch. Give it to Corporal Reed. Right now, you and me will take grave detail. Our boys don't deserve to rot in the sun like this."

Donovan slowly glanced around at the wreckage. He'd almost forgotten about the boys who hadn't made it. The ones whose bodies now littered the ground like trash. "Okay," the private finally replied.

Richards leaned in, placed a hand on Donovan's shoulder, and looked him in the eyes. "Mourn them later," said the sergeant. "Because if I'm right, this will all get really bad before it gets any better."

DEBRIEFING

38TH PARALLEL

YOU ARE NOW CROSSING
38TH PARALLEL
US C.O.B 728MP

HISTORY

Just days before the end of World War II, the Russian army entered Korea, which had been occupied by Japan. In an effort to stop their advancement, the U.S. War Department set the 38th parallel as a dividing line between the northern and southern half of the Korean peninsula. In 1950, the Russian-backed North Korean army attacked the south. The South Korean army, along with their U.S. allies, tried to stop them during three years of battles. Today, the 38th parallel still divides North and South Korea – and so do the ideas of communism and democracy.

QUICK FACTS

– The 38th parallel was first suggested as a dividing line as early as 1896.

– Neither North or South Korea approved the original demarcation line. It was established by the U.S. War Department.

– After the Korean War, the 38th parallel became known as the Demilitarized Zone (DMZ). This middle ground still separates the two countries.

– The DMZ stretches 162 miles across the Korean Peninsula. It is nearly 2.5 miles wide.

Fairchild C-119 Flying Boxcar

HISTORY

The Fairchild C-119 Flying Boxcar was an American military transport aircraft developed in the World War II era. It was designed to carry cargo, personnel (including wounded soldiers), and machinery. It could also drop cargo and paratroopers while in flight. The aircraft made its first flight in November 1947, and more than 1,100 C-119s had been built by 1955. The aircraft was commonly used during the Korean War as a transport for troops and equipment, and on several occasions, the C-119 was even used to drop portable bridges for personnel on the ground.

SPECIFICATIONS

CREW: 5
CAPACITY: 62 troops or 35 stretchers
LENGTH: 86 feet, 6 inches
WINGSPAN: 109 feet, 3 inches
HEIGHT: 26 feet 6 inches
EMPTY WEIGHT: 40,000 lbs.
LOADED WEIGHT: 64,000 lbs.
PAYLOAD: 10,000 lbs. of cargo
ENGINES: 2 x 3,500 horsepower engines
MAX SPEED: 296 mph
RANGE: 2,280 miles

CHAPTER 002

DISOBEDIENCE

Soon, the curtain of night had fallen. With no stars or moonlight, the area was blacker than a coal mine. The tree line was thirty yards from where the wreckage had scattered at the foot of the mountain. A large rip in the forest made by the aircraft's crash landing was bound to bring the enemy snooping around.

South Korea was a beautiful, mountainous country, filled with dense forests and rolling hills covered with whitecaps of snow and ice. It was also a harsh country, and the environment had taken its toll on everyone involved in the war. Extreme conditions and below-zero temperatures were killing American soldiers by the hundreds. The weather also made transporting gear and supplies to the front lines incredibly difficult.

But Private First Class Tony Donovan knew that, like his cousin Everett fighting at the nearby Chosin Reservoir, he must survive.

Looking south while he kept watch, Private Donovan tried to picture Everett, a U.S. Marine Corps Captain. He wondered if their platoon's failure to transport supplies would directly impact his cousin's situation. Donovan prayed this wasn't the case. However, he knew that every soldier counted on these resupply drops, and he felt a sense of personal failure.

Donovan shook it off. He scanned the tree line for any sign of human contact. He knew that it was only a matter of time before the Korean People's Army came to investigate the fire in the hills.

Meanwhile, a small man-made campfire crackled inside the dimpled tail section of the plane. A piece of the wing, propped over the opening of the compartment, created a makeshift door that covered the fire from outside view. Smoke floated skyward through a monstrous hole ripped in the ceiling from when they had crashed.

Huddled around a small map and compass, the corporals of the 249th Engineer Battalion assessed their situation with Sergeant Richards. Outside, PFC Donovan continued walking the perimeter, his new M1 Garand gripped in his hands.

"We're about fifty miles from the border, as far as I can tell," said Corporal DeLori, pointing at the map.

Reed rose, his arms crossed across his chest. "Ah, this is just stupid, Sergeant Richards," he grumbled. "Pilot's message or not, HQ's not going to send out a rescue team for us."

"Yeah, we're not important enough," said DeLori. "The Chosin Reservoir is about to explode, and they don't have time to look for five guys lost in the mountains. They're just gonna write us off. The new LT's gonna get us all killed, waiting out here like fish in a barrel."

"Hey! Like it or not, the man's is in charge," said Sergeant Richards. "He says left, we go left. It's that simple. There's a chain of command for a reason, for just this type of emergency."

But not everyone agreed.

Soares stood and paced. His cold, moist breath clouded the air. "That's baloney, Sarge, and you know it!" he finally exclaimed. "You were there in Europe, and you know most of these officers don't have a clue what they're doing."

"What do you suggest, Soares?" Sergeant Richards asked. "Should we disobey orders? Run off and leave the lieutenant here alone? Where are we gonna go?"

Richards glanced around at the other men. "You all trust me, right?" he asked.

The corporals nodded.

"Then trust me now," Richards said. "I'm not going to let anyone get killed out here. If rescue doesn't come by zero-seven, I'll reassess with the LT, but until then —"

"Intruder!" Donovan called from outside. The sudden sound of metal on metal echoed in the cabin, like rocks being hurled against the outer hull. Then came the sound of igniting gunpowder.

BANG! BANG!

"Move!" Richards shouted.

The soldiers jumped to their feet, rifles in hand. Richards kicked down the makeshift door, and he and the others emerged from the plane, weapons up and ready for a fight.

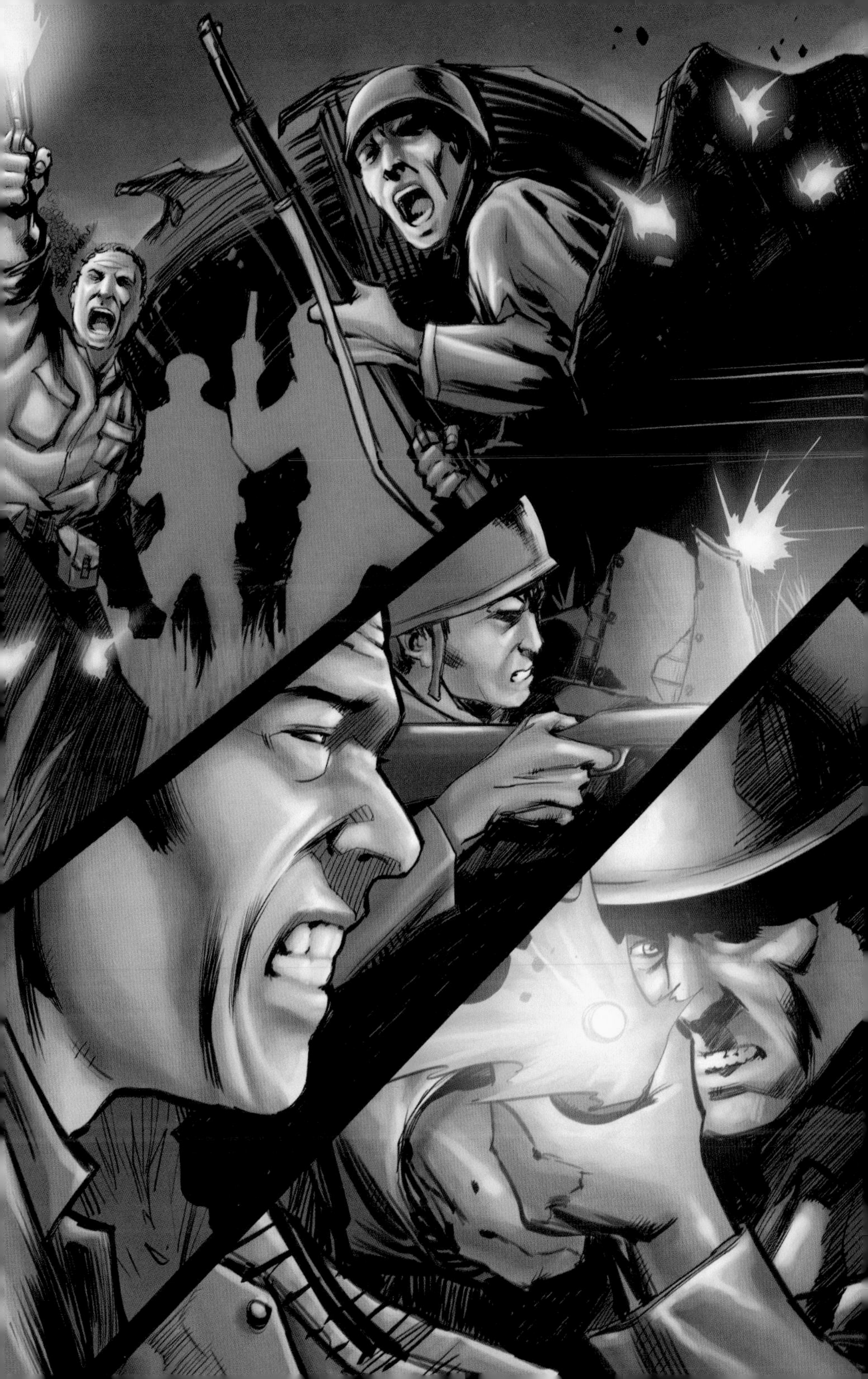

Private Donovan crouched behind a pallet of machine parts, taking cover from the enemy fire. "Contact at one o'clock," he yelled.

POP! POP! POP!

Quick flashes lit up the foliage in front of him. Two North Korean soldiers sliced through the tree line, taking potshots at the U.S. soldiers.

"Weapons free!" Richards commanded.

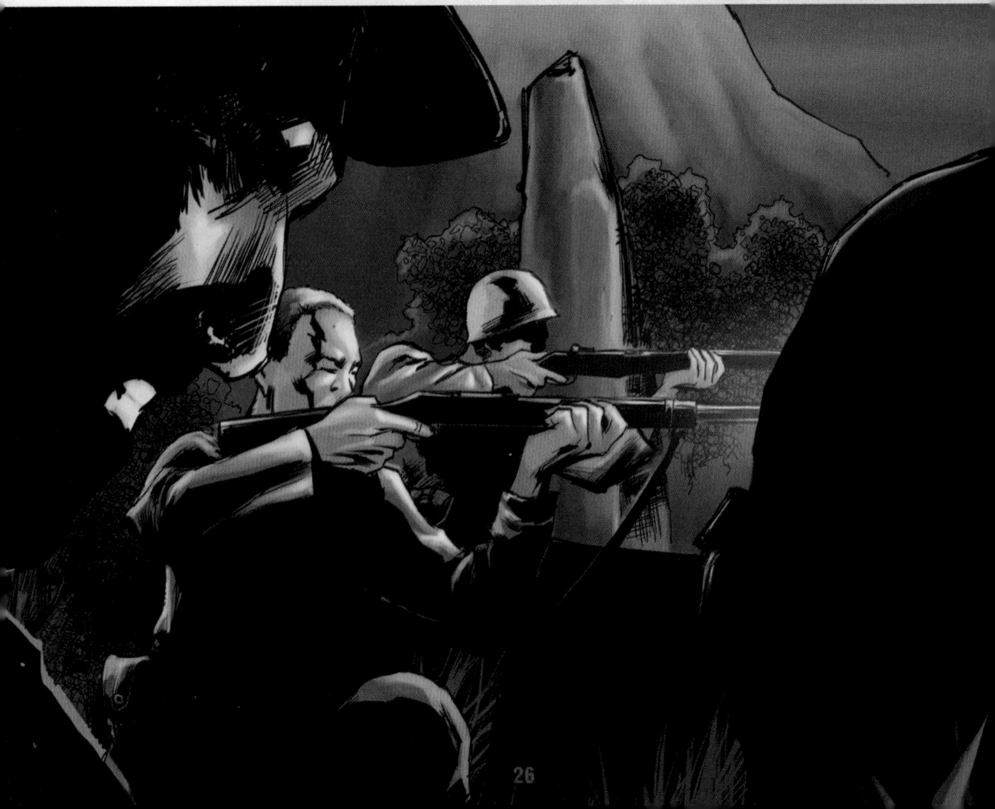

All five men spread out and returned fire at a rapid pace. Bullets flew through the air from both sides as leaves rustled in front of them.

The Koreans were on the move.

"They're up," DeLori shouted. He began to move in a crouch, flanking left.

"Covering fire!" Private Donovan yelled. The others concentrated their shots in a center mass, around the flashes in the trees.

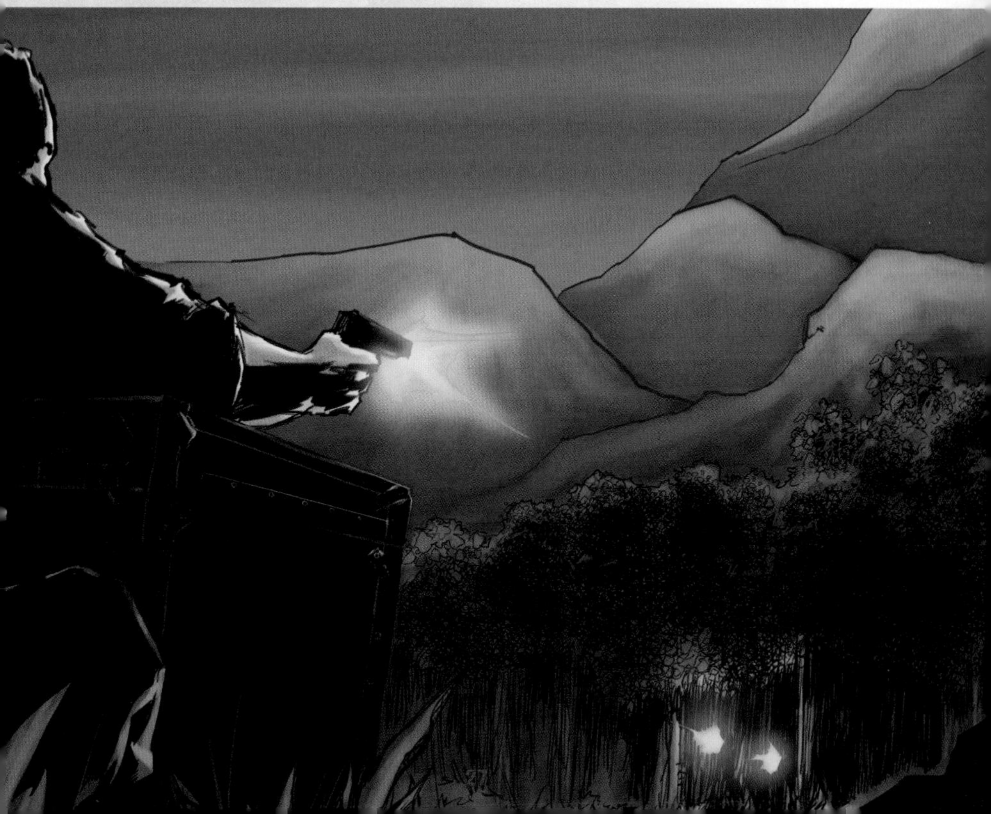

Breaking cover, DeLori headed toward the tree line, bullets chasing him and chipping up earth all the way. He took shelter behind a piece of metal debris from the crash site. Then he returned fire with his M1911 pistol.

One of the two Koreans fell to the ground, racked by bullets. Stuffing from his cold-weather uniform sprinkled the air around him.

The second Korean bolted, disappearing into the night. As he ran, the soldier pointed his 7.62mm Tokarev rifle behind him. He pulled the trigger wildly, trying his best to cover his escape.

The U.S. soldiers hit the dirt as the shots whizzed through the sky.

RATATAT! RATATA

Corporal DeLori jerked backward. He'd been hit. The slug flung him to the dirt in a heartbeat.

Richards rose and waved his hand in the air, giving the signal to stop shooting.

"Cease fire! Cease fire!" the sergeant shouted. "He's gone. Save your ammo, boys!"

"I'm hit!" yelled DeLori. He writhed on the ground in pain, clutching his shoulder.

Behind them, Lieutenant Polaski emerged from the main body of the crumpled wreck. He skinned his M1911 pistol from his holster and held it high in the air. "What have we got, Sergeant?" he asked, his eyes nervously scanning the darkness.

"Oh, man," mumbled Corporal Reed quietly. He shook his head in disgust and reloaded his M1 Garand with a new ammo magazine.

"Afraid you missed the party, sir," replied Sergeant Richards. He looked at his young leader with disgust. "But DeLori didn't. He's been hit."

Lieutenant Polaski turned his attention to Donovan. "You were on watch, Private!" the lieutenant shouted. "Why didn't you call?"

"I did, sir," Donovan said quietly.

"Well, I didn't hear it, Private," said the lieutenant.

"We all heard him, sir," said Sergeant Richards. "We ran out ASAP."

Kneeling at DeLori's side, Corporal Reed tried to calm his friend. "You're going to be okay, DeLori. Just relax," he said, peeling the blood-soaked uniform away from the corporal's wound.

Reed looked down at the bullet hole and grimaced. The bullet had entered DeLori's shoulder, bounced off of his collarbone, and exited his back — but not before piercing his right lung.

Corporal Reed turned to Sergeant Richards and shook his head slowly.

Richards looked at his commanding officer. "Sir —" he began.

"Don't, Sergeant! We're not abandoning this crash site!" Polaski ordered. He stepped up to Richards, locking eyes with the much larger sergeant.

Leathery and tan, with his strong jaw covered in stubble, Richards stood fast and calm. The younger, fresh-faced lieutenant stared at him with authority.

Sensing the tension, Donovan moved in. "With all due respect, sir, this is a losing battle," he said. "That was a Korean scouting party. Since we didn't kill both of them, that other KPA soldier is on his way to report what happened here."

"How do you know that, Private?" Polaski asked skeptically, keeping his eyes on Richards.

"That's what I'd do," Donovan answered.

Quietly, Polaski addressed Richards directly. "This is all your doing, trying to breed dissent in the ranks."

"You're new, Lieutenant," said the sergeant. "I get that. It's been a hard day. But if you ever question my loyalty again, I'll knock you on your butt. Sir."

Eyes wavering, Lieutenant Polaski broke off the staring match. He looked briefly over at his men. They were all scared and tired, and none of them knew what to do next.

"Look, sir," the sergeant said quietly. "These boys are engineers, not combat personnel. If the KPA comes down on us in numbers, we're gonna get slaughtered."

The lieutenant removed his helmet and wiped a hand over his crew-cut head. After a second, his shoulders dropped and his stance became less defensive. "We're not going to get far on foot, Sergeant," he said, "and both of the vehicles are smashed. What do you suggest?"

Richards shook his head. Donovan knew he didn't know what to say. But Donovan did. He'd been thinking about it since they landed. He decided to speak up.

"Actually, sir," Donovan said, "we could salvage what we can from the site. You know, take parts from each of the vehicles, and see if we can get one running."

Raising an eyebrow at Donovan, Richards grinned. Even the LT was impressed, but he was still unsure. "No," Polaski said. "SOP says we wait."

Sergeant Richards eyed his commanding officer. "Sir, at least let them try," Richards said. "It'll keep morale up while we wait. If they can make it work, it'll be a good plan B."

Polaski was visibly frustrated. Donovan could tell he was tired of this conversation. The lieutenant waved them off.

"Fine, but just as a backup plan," said the lieutenant. "And on their own time."

Smiling, Richards nodded over to Donovan.

The private took off running. For the first time since the crash, he felt a sense of purpose.

NORTH KOREAN SOLDIERS

HISTORY

In 1950, the North Korean army, also known as the Korean People's Army (KPA), was heavily armed and well trained. During their initial attacks on the south, 100,000 KPA soldiers easily overcame South Korean troops and overtook the city of Seoul. However, as the war continued with U.S. support, the KPA suffered heavy losses. By the end of the Korean War, the KPA had lost more then 290,000 soldiers in less than three years. Today, the KPA remains intact, led by the Supreme Commander Kim Jong-il.

COMMUNISM

North Korea, officially known as the Democratic People's Republic of Korea (DPRK), is a communist country. The government owns all of the land, businesses, and houses, and citizens cannot vote for their leaders. In the United States, leaders are elected by the people, and citizens can buy houses and other items with the money they earn. This type of government is called a democracy. The differences between these views helped lead to the Korean War.

U.S. TROOPS IN KOREA

HISTORY

When North Korea invaded South Korea on June 25, 1950, U.S. President Harry Truman spoke with his Joint Chief of Staff, Omar Bradley. Truman and Bradley agreed to "draw the line" on the advancement of communist governments like Russia and North Korea. On June 27, they committed air and naval support and promised U.S. troops as part of an "international peacekeeping force." During the next three years, more than 5.7 million U.S. soldiers would serve as part of the mission to keep North Korea on their side of the 38th parallel.

OMAR BRADLEY

Omar N. Bradley (1893-1981) served as the first chairman of the U.S. Joint Chiefs of Staff.

CHAPTER 003

AD-HOC

It had been the longest night of Donovan's life. He and Corporal Reed had performed surgery on the dying jeep, transplanting one metal organ for another. The men had taken turns between walking the perimeter and turning a wrench.

Now, the sun was beginning to rise over the scene of destruction. No one was sure if they'd get a heartbeat out of their Frankensteined jeep.

"Hand me the crescent wrench, will you?" Corporal Reed asked Donovan.

Donovan found the tool and slapped it into Reed's hand.

"Shine some light in here," Reed ordered.

Donovan produced a brass WWI-era trench lighter and sparked the flint.

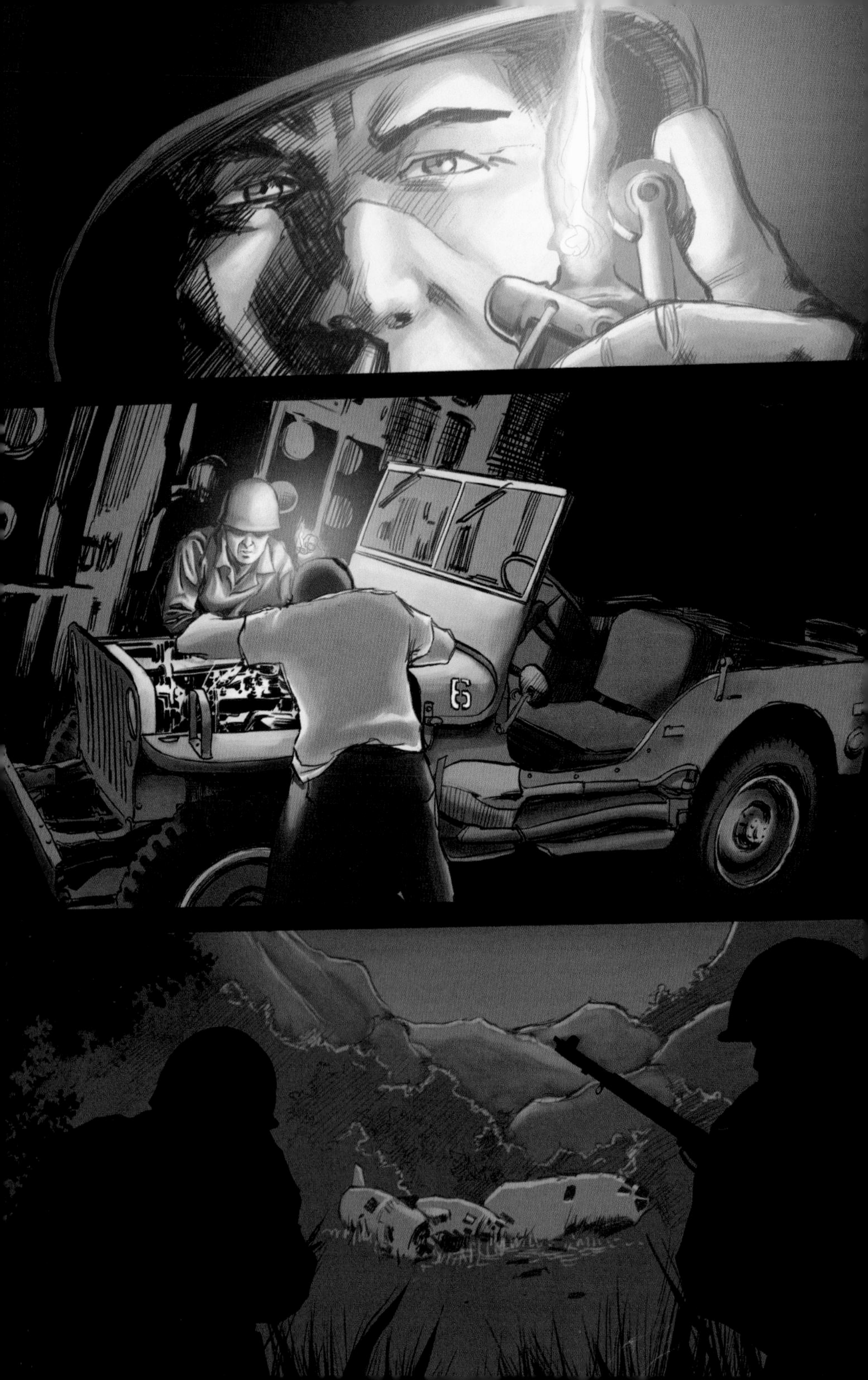

"Nice antique," Reed said with a smile. "Where'd that come from?"

"My cousin," Donovan answered. "He got this in WWII from a British soldier. Said it always kept him out of harm's way on his missions during the war. He gave it to me to keep me safe."

Reed nodded and smiled again, this time, sadly. "Guess its lucky powers don't extend to other wars."

"We ain't dead yet, Reed!" Sergeant Richards's voice boomed into the plane's main fuselage. He strode inside, his rifle slung over his shoulder. "How's it coming?" he asked the men.

Standing and wiping grease from his hands, Private Donovan looked at the jeep and shrugged. "They're pretty tough crackers, Sarge," he said. "Both engine cases took anti-aircraft fire when we were shot down. We've spent the night replacing headers, pistons, and filling any holes with spit and gum."

"Will she run?" asked Richards bluntly.

"Yeah," answered Donovan. "I think."

"How long until we can blow this Popsicle stand?" Richards asked.

"I dunno." Donovan scratched his head. "Another hour, give or take."

"Good," said Richards.

"Wait, Sarge," Donovan said. "I'm just saying she'll start. I have no idea how long she'll run."

"It's gonna have to do, Private," said Richards.

*   *   *

"That's good to hear," said Polaski after Sergeant Richards had given him the news. The lieutenant looked into the sky and then back down at his watch.

Adjusting the rifle sling on his shoulder, Richards looked at his CO and shook his head. "Sir, it's been over twenty-four hours," Richards said. "If KPA was coming, they'd been here by now."

"Maybe so," Polaski said.

"But DeLori," continued Richards, "he ain't gonna last much longer. And I know he'd rather go out fighting than just sitting around and dying."

The lieutenant rose. "You're right," he said. "I'm sorry I didn't listen to you sooner, Richards. Let's get the men to gather up what they can. We're getting out of here —"

KABLAMO!!

A sound like a small thunderclap echoed through the air. Red liquid, thick as syrup, sprayed from the lieutenant's neck and splattered Richards' face.

Eyes wide in surprise, Lieutenant Polaski gasped for breath. He stuck a hand out to support himself. But he missed the Sergeant's shoulder. Then he crumpled, his knees buckling below him.

"Lieutenant!" Richards screamed, dropping to the side of his commanding officer.

Private Donovan came running from inside the wreck. He stumbled, fell, and then crawled to the pair.

Small bubbles popped from Polaski's mouth. The blood in his throat made a gurgling sound every time he tried to breath.

"What happened —?!" But Donovan stopped short as round after round of enemy gunfire ripped up the dirt around them.

"G-g-go!" Polaski managed to spit out.

With a quivering hand, the LT tried to pull his pistol from its holster, but he just wasn't strong enough.

Sergeant Richards pulled the gun from its cowhide sheath. Then he handed the .45-caliber pistol to his CO and nodded.

Polaski held the weapon in the air and squeezed the trigger. A few rounds ripped into the trees. It was a last-ditch effort at covering fire as Donovan and Richards ran for the fuselage, bullets hunting them all the way.

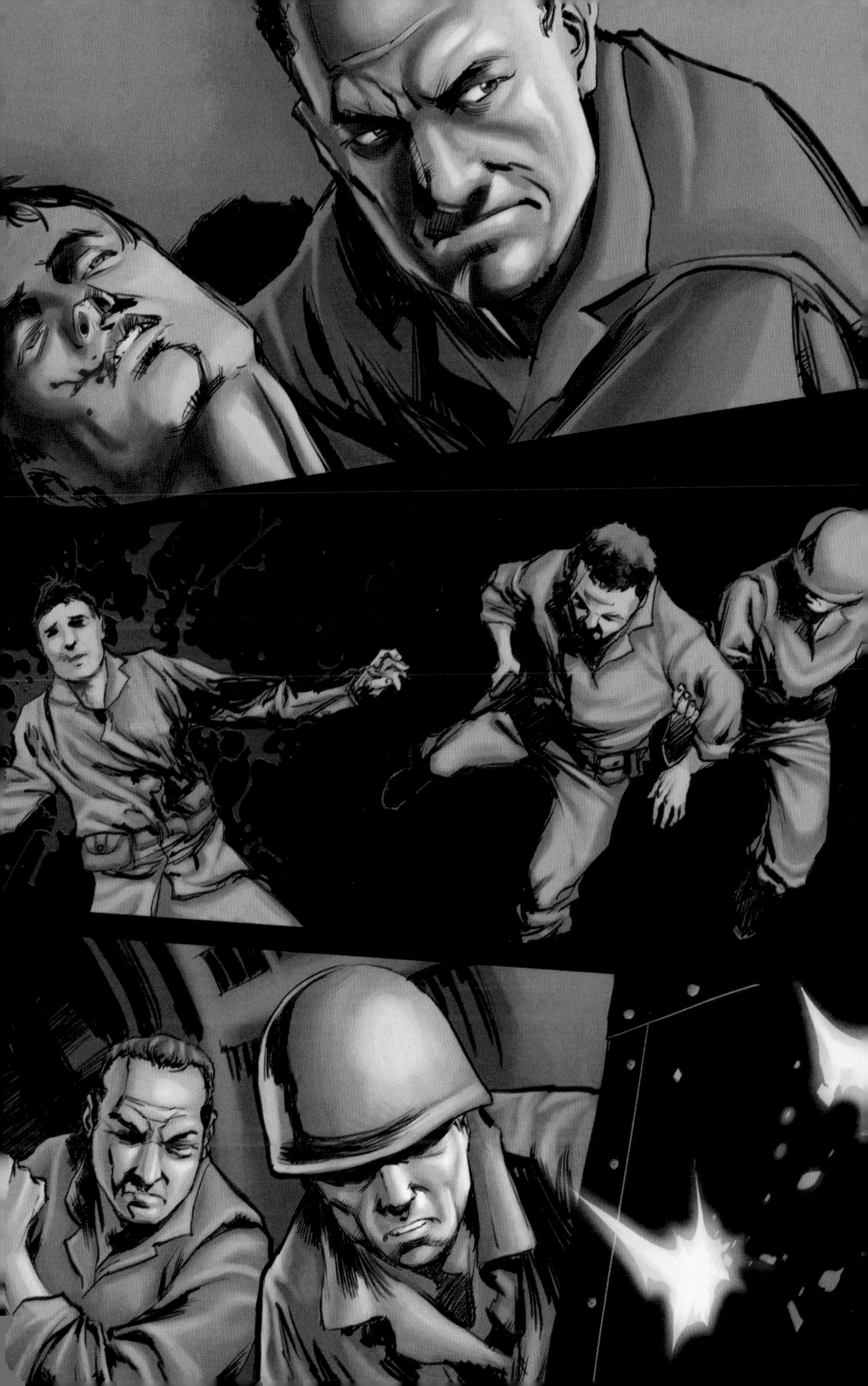

About fifty yards away from the crash site, an entire platoon of thirty-five KPA soldiers were spread out in the bushes. They quickly advanced on the five remaining American soldiers.

The enemies moved swiftly, their triggers depressed and empty brass casings spitting out of their weapons' ejection ports.

W!POW!POW!PO

Bullets zinged and whipped through the forest. They peppered the crash site and found their way into the fallen body of Lieutenant Polaski — a cruel end to the young man's tour of duty.

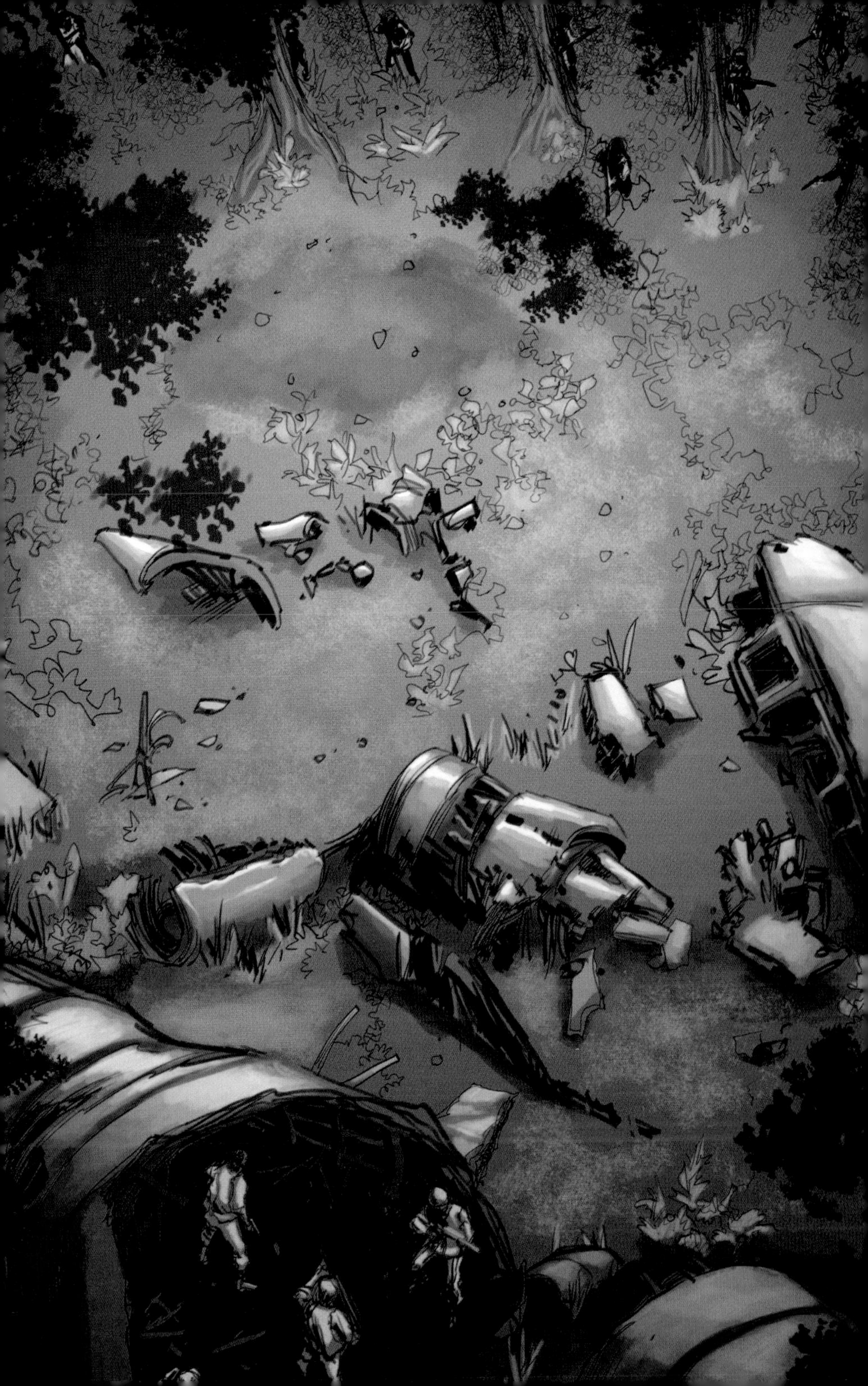

DEBRIEFING

CHOSIN RESERVOIR CAMPAIGN

SPECIFICATIONS

DATES: November 27–December 13, 1950
LOCATION: Chosin Reservoir, North Korea
MILITARY STRENGTH:
United Nations (South Korea, United Kingdom, United States): 30,000 troops
Chinese: 60,000 troops

FACT

The 30,000 UN soldiers who fought during the Battle of Chosin Reservoir in North Korea are often nicknamed the "The Frozen Chosin" or "The Chosin Few."

HISTORY

At the end of 1950, Chinese forces, known as the People's Volunteer Army (PVA), attacked U.S. X Corps soldiers in the northeastern part of North Korea. Soon, 30,000 UN troops were surprised and surrounded by more than double the amount of PVA soldiers. During the next seventeen days, UN soldiers (which included troops from South Korea, the United Kingdom, and the United States) endured harsh conditions and fought their way out of the trap. In the process, the UN was forced out of North Korea. However, the brutal battle left the Chinese forces crippled.

DEADLY CONDITIONS

HISTORY

One of the deadliest forces facing soldiers during the Korean War wasn't enemy troops; it was the weather. More than 6 million troops, or 90% of the soldiers serving during the war, suffered some form of frostbite. Those who fought in the Battle of Chosin Reservoir were particularly hard hit. Temperatures in the mountains of North Korea dipped to lower than 30 degrees below zero during the battle. With inadequate gear, thousands lost fingers and toes to the subzero temps; many others lost their lives.

COLD GEAR

At the beginning of the Korean War, U.S. soldiers wore similar uniforms to those worn in World War II. However, after suffering injuries and losses to frostbite during the first winter in North Korea, the military adopted cold-weather gear. These items included the M1951 Parka, Mitten Shells, Trouser Shells, and the M1951 Winter Pile Hat. They also added insulated boots, which soldiers dubbed "Mickey Mouse Boots," for their extra large size.

CHAPTER 004

HOPE

The corporals rushed toward the opening of the fuselage. At the same time, Donovan and Richards came storming in, bullets bird-dogging their footsteps.

"What's happening?" asked Corporal Reed, nervously popping a bubble of gum against his lips.

Suddenly, shots splattered the hull from all sides. The soldiers ducked and dropped to the deck.

"Answer your question?" Donovan muttered. He crawled, belly to the ground, toward their jeep.

Sergeant Richards looked up and finally saw his men's handiwork. Several pieces of the plane's hull had been bolted to the exterior of the jeep. With the makeshift armor screwed into the body, the vehicle looked like a heavy-duty M1 Scout car.

"I'm impressed, boys," said the sergeant.

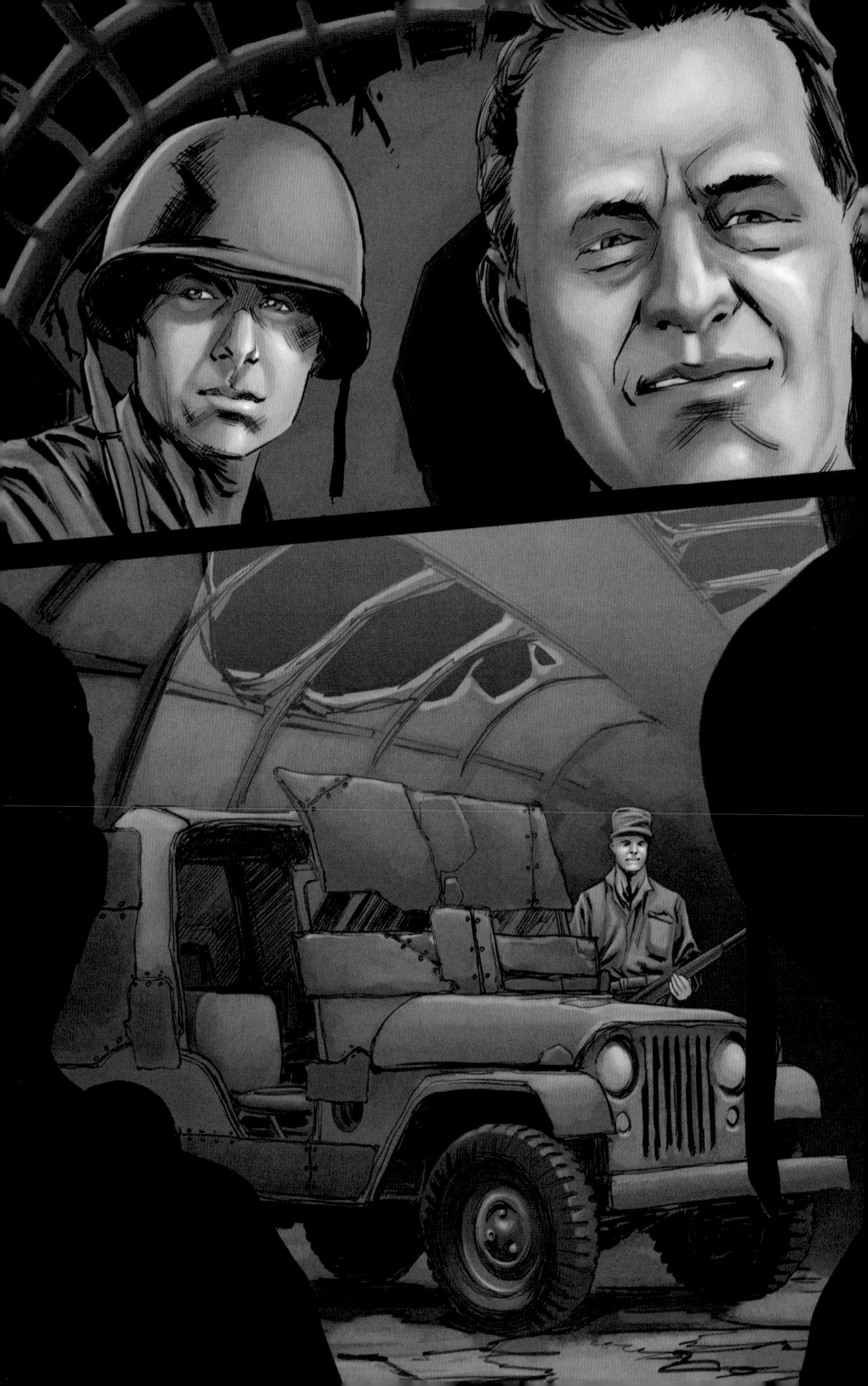

Then the sergeant looked down at the wounded DeLori. "Is he ready?" Richards asked Corporal Soares.

The corporal finished putting the last of the morphine into DeLori's arm and nodded.

Smiling, Richards leaned in and spoke to DeLori softly. "We're leaving, kid," he said.

DeLori understood.

The men lifted him onto the standby stretcher made from blouses and piping from the plane.

"And the LT?" asked DeLori quietly as they placed him in the rear quarter of the transport and strapped him in with the seatbelts.

Everyone froze at the question.

"He's gonna be watching our back, pal," Donovan lied. "Just rest and hang on."

Bouncing into the front passenger seat, Soares yelled, "Shotgun!"

"You know that means you're in charge of protecting the driver, right, kid?" Richards said smugly.

Glancing around nervously, Corporal Soares jumped out and let Richards have the front seat.

"Right, you better take it then," the corporal mumbled.

Sergeant Richards sat, placed a foot on the A-frame for support, and loaded his rifle. Donovan slid into the driver's seat beside him. The private placed a hand on the ignition key and said a silent prayer.

He turned the key.

CLICK!

Nothing happened.

Letting out an exasperated sigh, Donovan sprung from his seat, popped open the hood, and looked inside. "Reed, you and Soares cover the door!" he ordered.

After running to the front of the plane, the two men crouched behind old crates. They opened fire, trying their best to buy some time. Outside, the KPA were advancing on the tree line, firing blindly at the site. They were a mere twenty yards away from them.

Under the jeep's hood, Donovan quickly spotted the problem. A small amount of fuel was leaking from the fuel line. It had been hit by a stray bullet. Donovan looked around the cabin for something to fix it with, but there wasn't anything in sight. "All I need is some tape, or something sticky —"

The idea hit him like a land mine.

"Reed!" yelled Donovan.

ANG! BANG! BANG

Popping shots from his M1 Garand, Reed didn't look back. "Little busy, Private!" he shouted.

"You got a stick of that Beeman's gum?" Donovan yelled to the corporal.

"Just the one in my mouth!" Reed yelled back.

"That'll do," Donovan said.

"But it's my last piece!" Reed protested.

Suddenly, a Korean soldier sprung up in front of Reed. The enemy thrust his bayoneted rifle toward the corporal's chest.

BANG!

A sudden shot came from inside the fuselage. It struck the Korean and sent him reeling backward.

Sergeant Richards racked the action on his rife and glared at Reed. "Give him the gum!" Richards ordered.

Corporal Reed reached into his mouth and threw Donovan his chewed-up bubble gum.

The young private caught the sticky wad. He spread it out like taffy, carefully wrapped it around the fuel line, and pressed it tightly.

Donovan jumped back into the jeep, Donovan tried the key again. This time, thick clouds of black smoke belched from the exhaust pipe as the jeep tried to return to life. Chugging and rattling, the jeep turned over!

ROOOOOM!

"Punch it, Donovan!" Richards ordered.

Donovan slipped the jeep into first gear. As it rolled out, Corporals Reed and Soares leaped into the back.

After exploding from the fuselage, the up-armored jeep sped down the embankment. It took heavy fire from the KPA as they advanced out of the trees.

Two Koreans tried to rush the jeep, but Reed hammered out. He butt-stroked him across the face with his rifle as they drove off.

Bullets ricocheted off the makeshift armor, but the cleverness of the American soldiers had paid off. They were on their way to safety.

*   *   *

Trees whipped by them at fifty miles per hour. Eventually, the men felt they were far enough away from the KPA troops to finally relax a bit.

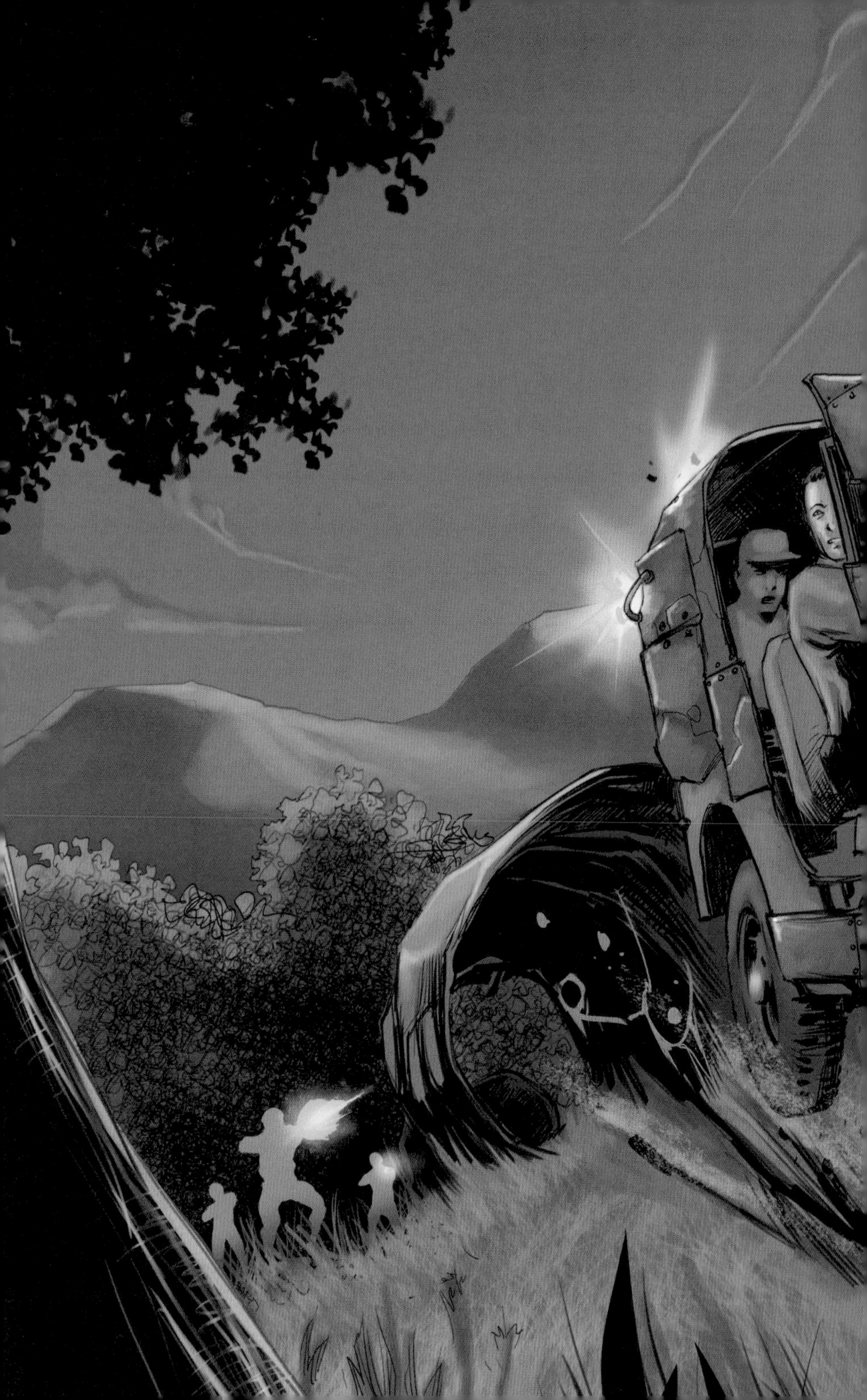

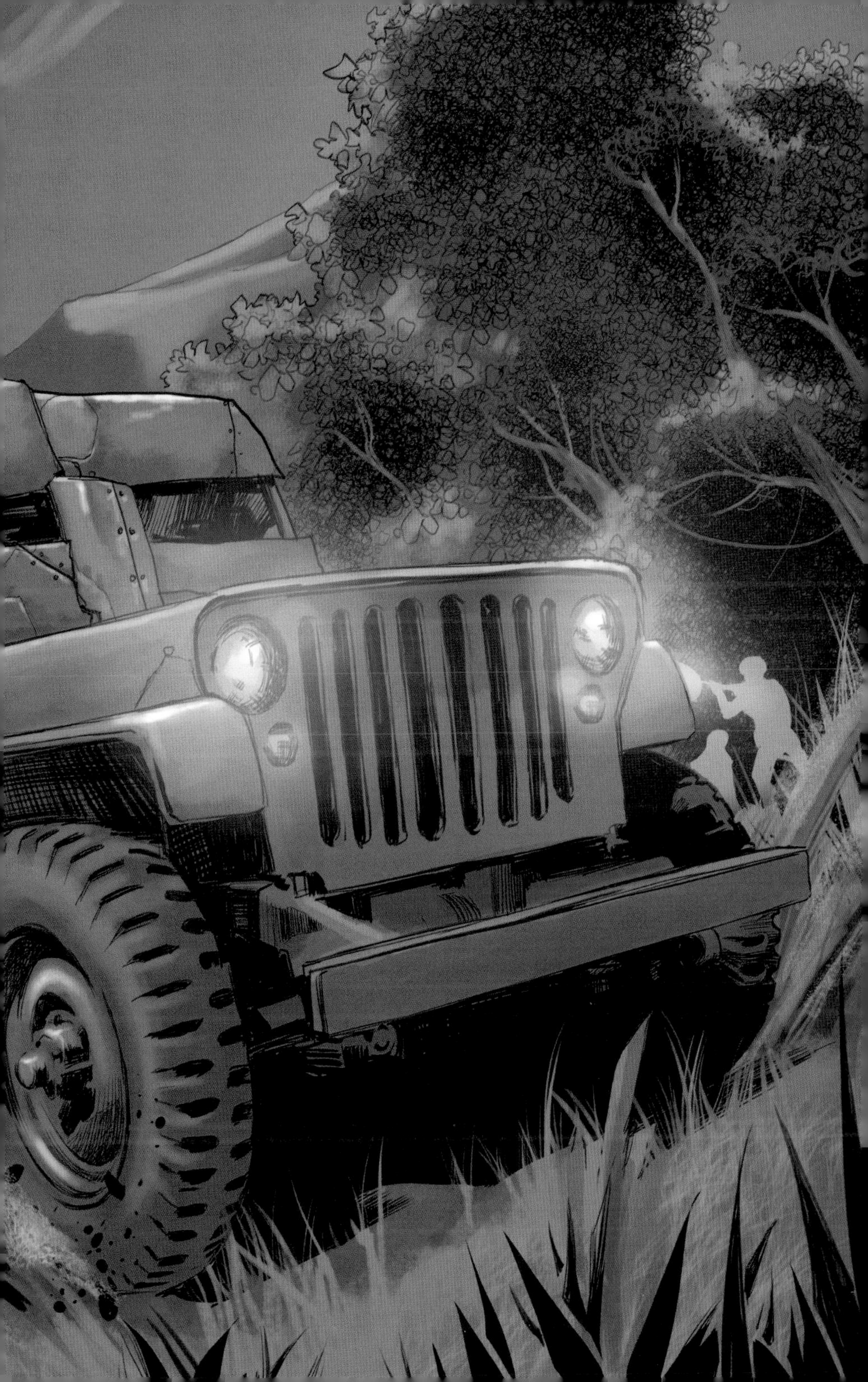

"Where the heck am I going, Sarge?" Donovan yelled over to Richards.

The sergeant was urgently trying to read a small map in his lap as they bounced along the road. "We're headin' south, and that's good!" he said. "We were —"

POP! POP! POP!

Bullets zipped in through the windshield. Glass shattered into the front seat and cut the sergeant under his left eye.

Appearing like a ghost, a Chinese carrier truck squealed onto the road. It kicked up dirt and rocks as it slid in behind them, gaining quickly.

"Vehicle from the rear!" yelped Corporal Reed. He tried taking aim on the bumpy road.

He and Corporal Soares pulled their triggers as quickly as they could. Meanwhile, Donovan slammed on the gas, doing his best to keep the jeep ahead of the truck.

But the enemy troops kept advancing.

"Hang on, boys!" Donovan shouted.

Reed and Soares held DeLori tight.

Donovan turned the wheel again, but this time, the jeep's nose was suddenly pointing down a steep decline. They were headed straight down the side of a dirt-covered mountain.

"This is gonna get rough!" said the private.

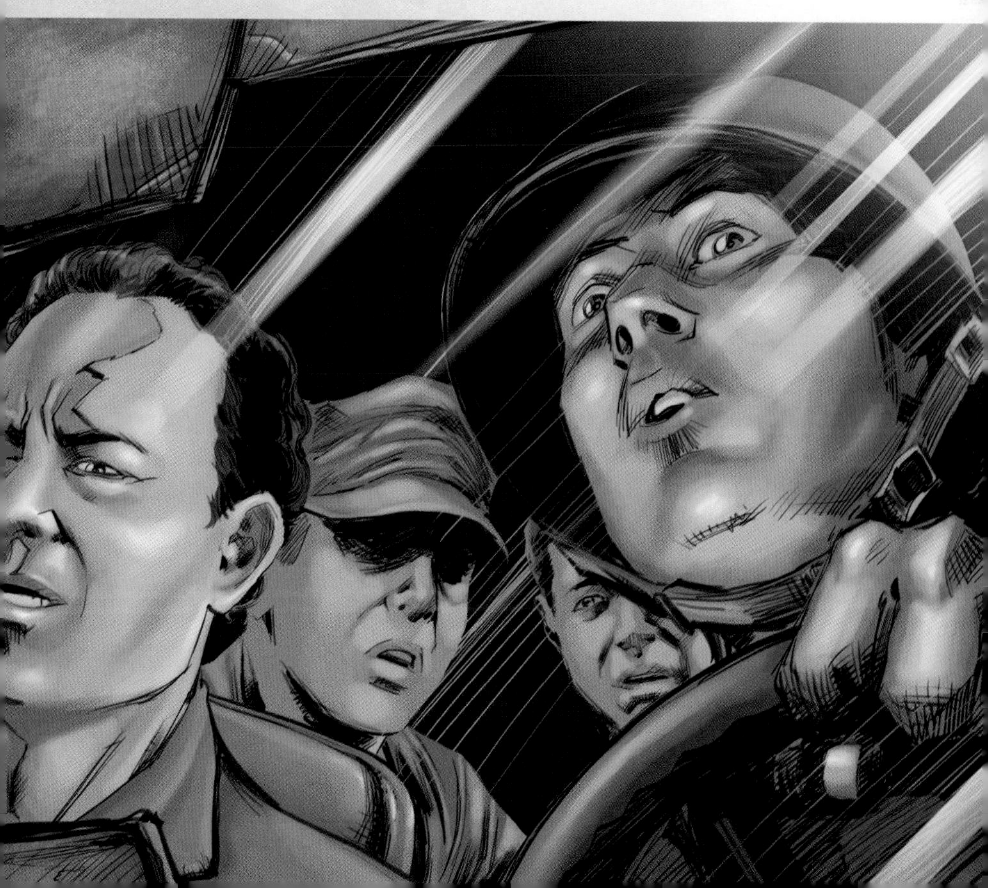

M4 SHERMAN TANK

SPECIFICATIONS

SERVICE: 1942-1955
LENGTH: 19 feet 2 inches
WIDTH: 8 feet 7 inches
HEIGHT: 9 feet
WEIGHT: 66,800 lbs.
SPEED: 25-30 mph
RANGE: 120 miles
ACCOMMODATION: 5 crew
members (commander, gunner,
loader, driver, co-driver)

FACT

A device called a gyrostabilizer
allowed the M4's 75-mm gun to
fire accurately on the move.

HISTORY

The United States built nearly 50,000
M4, or Medium Tanks, during World
War II. The M4 Sherman, named
after Civil War Union General William
Tecumseh Sherman, quickly became
an effective weapon for the U.S.
and other Allied forces. The M4 was
reliable, easy to maintain, and fast. Its
main 75-mm gun could fire accurately
in any direction, even while moving.
Unfortunately, this weapon could not
penetrate the armor of heavier tanks,
such as the German Panther and
Tiger. Even so, the M4 remained an
important vehicle in the U.S. military
for years to come.

M1911 PISTOL

SPECIFICATIONS

SERVICE: 1911-present
DESIGNER: John M. Browning
WEIGHT: 2.44 lbs.
LENGTH: 8.25 inches
BARREL: 5.03 inches
HISTORY: First used by the U.S. Army on March 29, 1911, the M1911 pistol quickly became a popular weapon for all branches of the U.S. military. The single-action, semi-automatic handgun fired .45-caliber cartridges from a seven-round magazine. During WWII, the U.S. government purchased 1.9 million M1911s. They remained a vital weapon throughout the Korean War.

M1 Garand

Developed by John C. Garand, the M1 rifle was adopted by the U.S. Army in 1936. It was the first semi-automatic rifle used by soldiers and quickly became the most popular.

CHAPTER 005

FASTER!

The jeep jerked like a bucking bronco as it descended over the lip of the mountain. The men desperately tried to hang on.

In the back, Corporal DeLori opened his eyes and smiled. "We at Coney Island, Pete?" he joked.

With one hand clutching his helmet and the other holding his wounded friend, Soares couldn't help but laugh. "Almost there, pal!" he said.

Finally, the jeep settled at the bottom of the hill and headed south again, leaving the befuddled KPA troops at the top of the hill.

Or so they thought.

KABLAMO!!

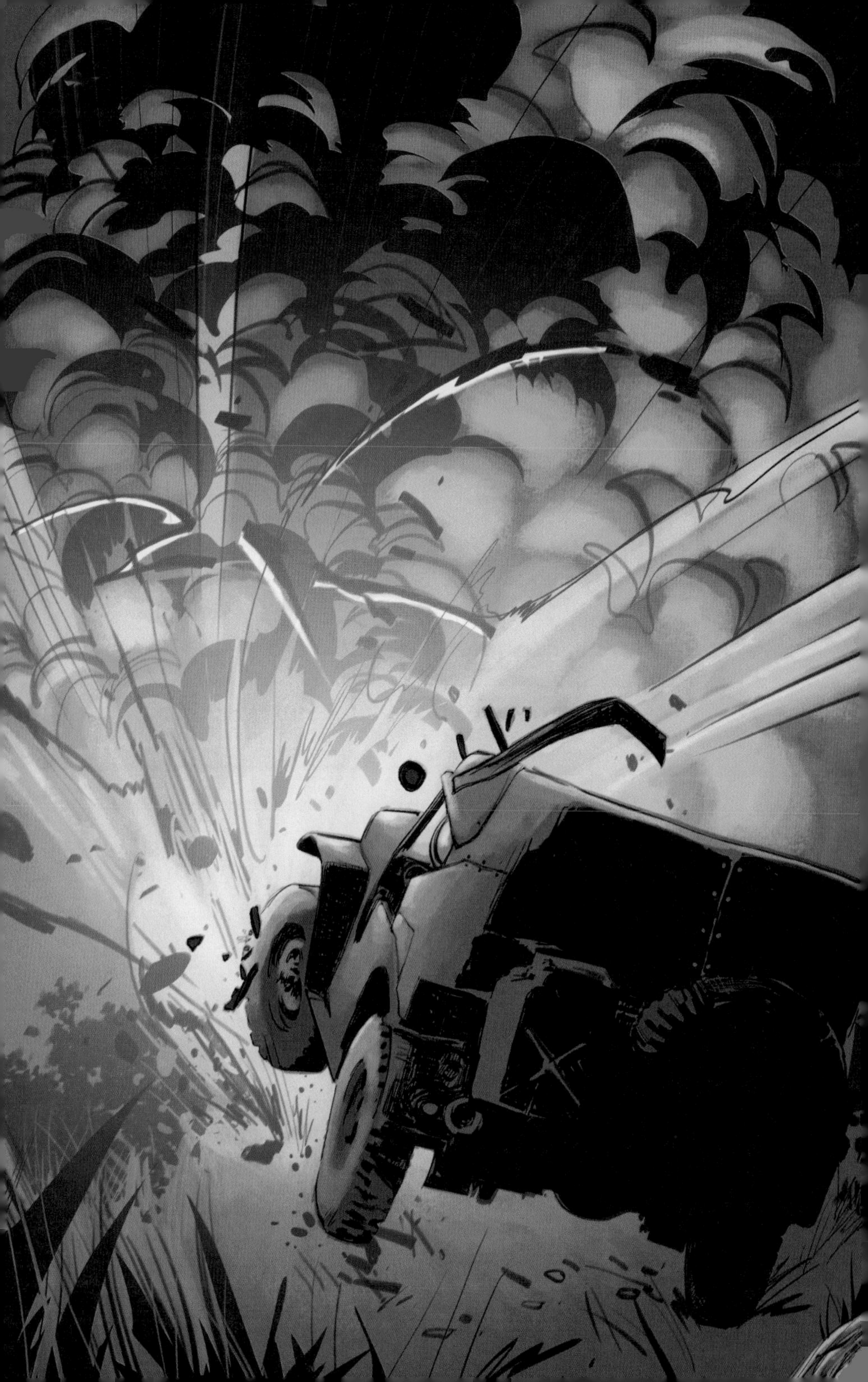

A massive explosion rocked the ground to the right of the jeep, almost flipping them over. A shower of dirt and rocks rained from the sky. It sprinkled down on the soldiers as a tremendous crater appeared in the ground.

All the men turned to see a metal behemoth crashing through the forest, collapsing trees like toothpicks. An IS-3 Iosif Stalin tank crashed onto the road behind them.

It fired again.

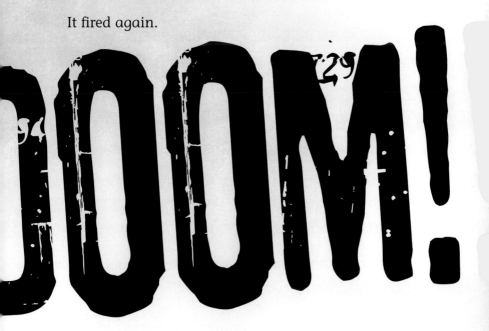

Weaving right, the jeep just missed the tank shell as it impacted with the ground. The tank began to give chase as it roared off after them.

"Fast, Donovan! Faster!" Richards yelled as he, Soares, and Reed fired at the tank.

Their aim was true, but the shots were useless. They bounced right off the tank's armored hull.

Donovan swerved the vehicle, doing what he could to avoid being targeted. But the action just made it harder for his men to take accurate shots.

From the top of the tank, the main gun hatch popped open and a KPA soldier emerged. Taking the machine gun handles in his hand, he opened up on the jeep.

Thick, chunky shots echoed out of the anti-aircraft gun. Rounds sped through the air, impacting the ground all around the jeep. Though it had a slower rate of fire than most machine guns, the projectiles still did their jobs. They pierced the jeep's hull.

Inside, the U.S. soldiers yo-yoed back and forth, doing everything to hang on for dear life.

"Take that sucker out, Sergeant!" Private Donovan yelled. He ducked as searing hot lead zipped past his ears at subsonic speeds.

Sergeant Richards placed his elbow on his knee and the barrel of his weapon against his seat back. He steadied the weapon the best he could.

Then he squeezed the trigger.

Suddenly, the tanker gunner's head snapped back like it'd been hit with a baseball bat. However, the enemy soldier's fingers were still wrapped tightly around the firing mechanism. As the KPA soldier slumped over his weapon, bullets flew wildly through the air.

One lucky shot from the dead soldier's gun blew out the jeep's front tire.

The jeep's rear wheels left the road, kicked up, and flipped over into the air. Rolling left, the jeep flew for a few feet, but crashed down hard on its side and ground to a halt in the heavy dirt road.

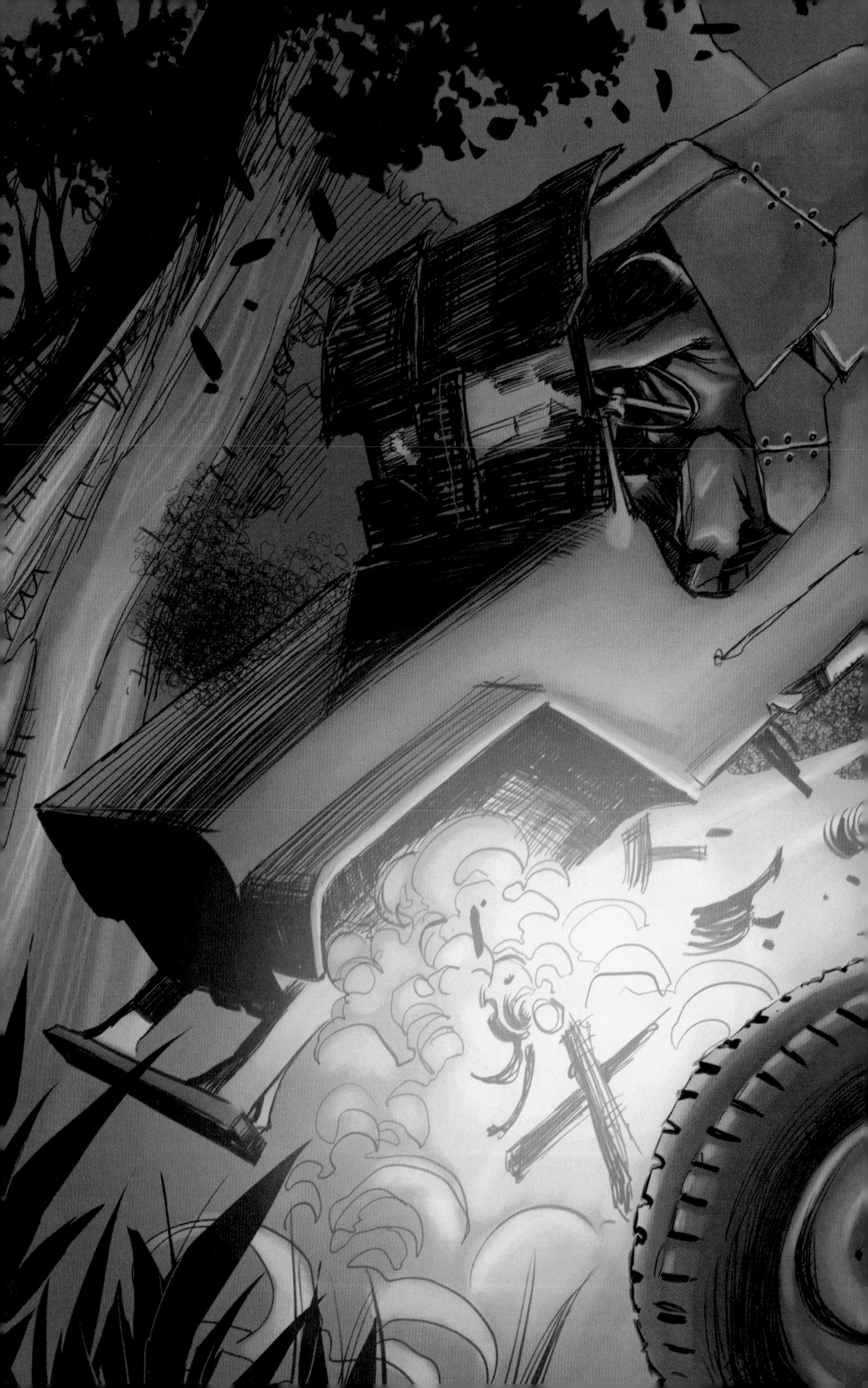

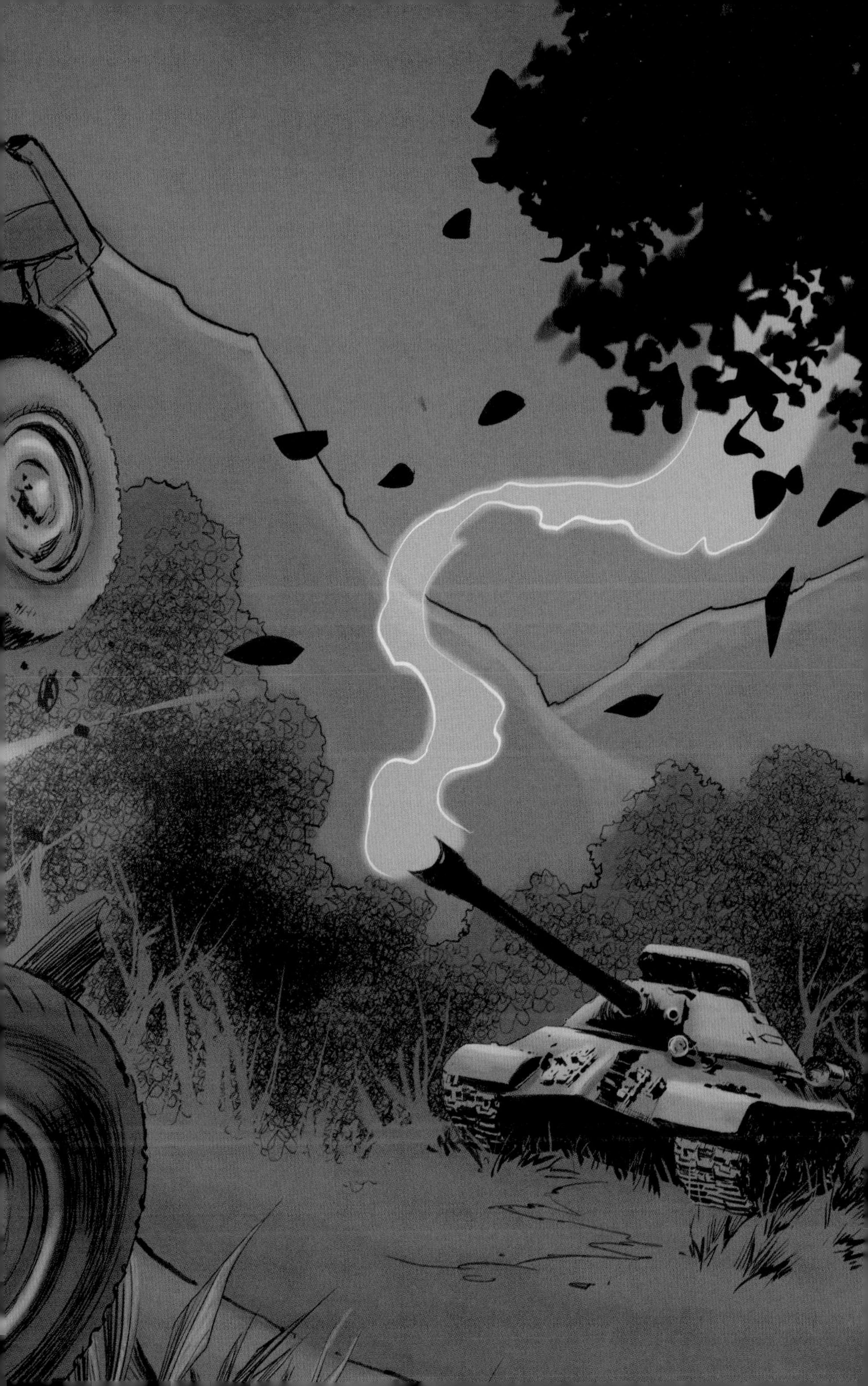

Behind them, the tank stopped and, for an instant, all was quiet.

The men in the jeep had survived, but looked worse for wear. Donovan, still behind the wheel, looked over and saw Reed. The corporal was lying behind the cover of the wreck, about three yards away. Richards was in the passenger seat, and DeLori was straight up, still strapped into his stretcher.

Corporal Soares was trapped under the jeep. His legs were pinned between the road and the transport, and he was unconscious.

"Another crash landing," Reed grumbled. He rose slowly and grabbed up his rifle.

Springing to life, Richards grabbed Soares' rifle and shoved it into Donovan's hands.

"We ain't done yet," Richards said as he stood, taking aim over the jeep.

Reed covered the backside of the jeep. Donovan crouched over the hood, peeking around the front quarter of the vehicle.

A sudden mechanical clicking sound filled the air. The enemy tank's turret swung in their direction. Its D25-T 122-mm gun ratcheted down toward its target.

Swallowing hard, Richards knew none of them would ever see home again.

"Gents," Sergeants Richards said, looking around at his men. "It was a pleasure serving with you." He smiled and racked the action on his M1 Garand.

Reed smiled back and nodded. "We all gotta go sometime."

"Let's make it count," Donovan said. He grinned and readied his weapon.

"Fire —!" Richards ordered.

Just then, the tank exploded!

A massive ball of orange flame and searing heat rose into the air. Fragments of the KPA tank's armor plating flew through the sky, slamming against the underside of the jeep and causing the men to duck for cover.

For an instant, all three men shared a dazed and confused look of disbelief.

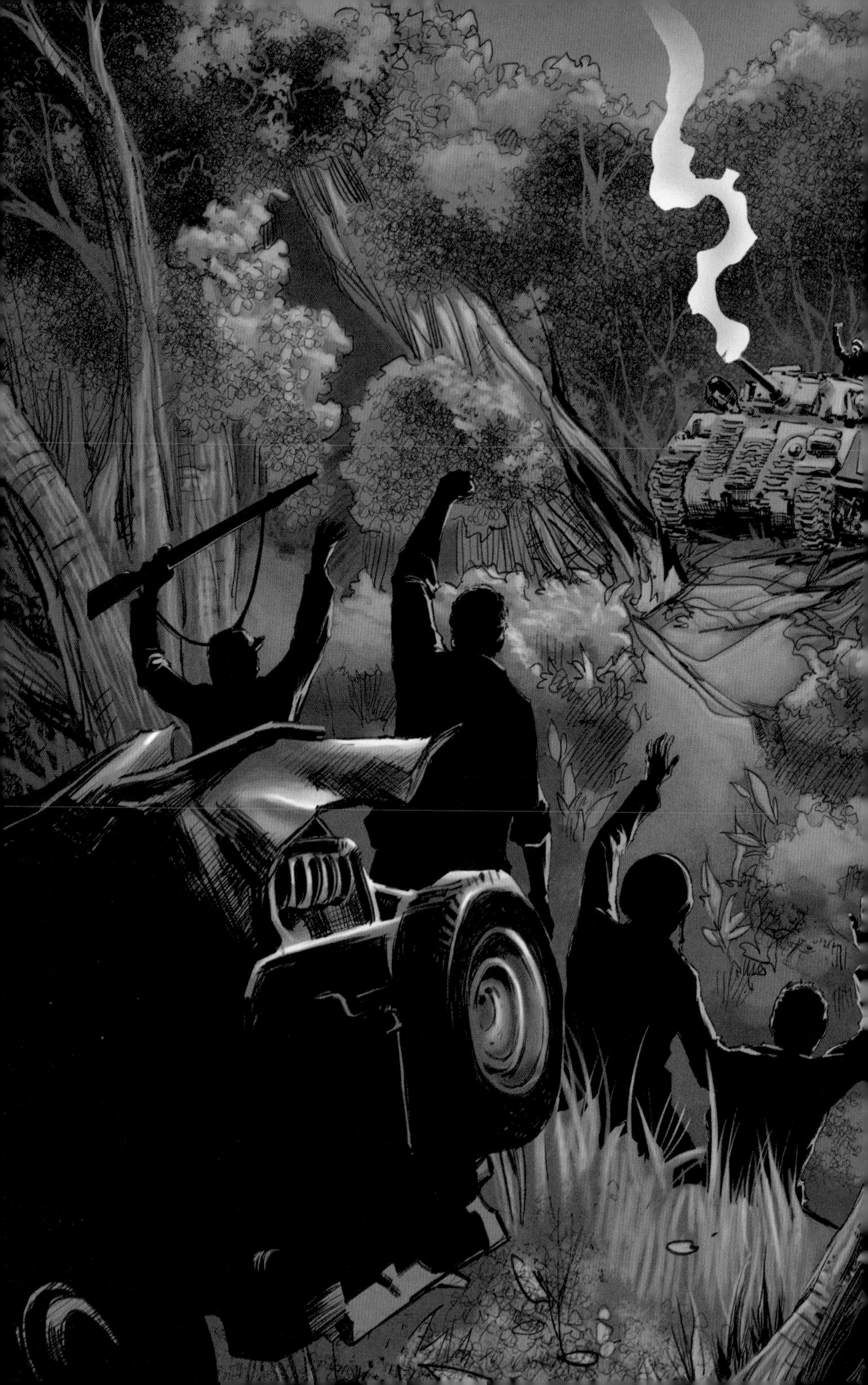

"How?" Donovan asked, but Richards shook his head.

Corporal Reed glanced behind him, and instantly a smile blasted across his face.

"Look!" he yelled as he pointed to their rear.

Into the clearing, an M4 Sherman tank was rolling up on their position. Its 75-mm gun was smoking.

Looking at Donovan and Reed, Sergeant Richards smiled. "Boys, we're going home," he said.

DEBRIEFING

CASUALTIES OF THE KOREAN WAR

STATISTICS

Casualty statistics vary widely. However, many soldiers paid the ultimate price during the Korean War. Below are some historical estimates:

COUNTRY	TOTAL DEATHS
China	100,000–900,000
North Korea	520,000
South Korea	420,000
UN Allies	16,0000
United States	36,940

WAR MEMORIAL

Dedicated on July 27, 1995, the Korean War Veterans Memorial in Washington, D.C., honors those who fought and died in the Korean War. Operated by the National Park Service, the memorial features a 164-foot-long granite wall, etched with the photos of 2,500 U.S. troops. The memorial also features 19 stainless steel statues, each standing 7 feet 3 inches tall. These statues commemorate a squad on patrol and represent members from each branch of the Armed Forces. More than 3 million people visit each year.

SURRENDER

HISTORY

Although negotiations for a cease fire began on July 10, 1951, fighting on the Korean Peninsula continued for two more years. Finally, on July 27, 1953, all sides agreed to end the conflict. As part of the agreement, the parties formed a middle ground called Korean Demilitarized Zone (DMZ). Running along the 38th parallel, this 160-mile-long border area still separates the two countries. It is nearly 2.5 miles wide and monitored by armed guard on both sides. The buffer zone also includes a Joint Security Area, used for negotiations since 1953.

AFTERMATH

Today, the DMZ still divides the Korean Peninsula. South Korea, officially known as Republic of Korea, remains an independent nation with a democratic republic system of government, which is similar to the U.S. government. North Korea, or Democratic People's Republic of Korea, remains a communist country. It is led by Kim Jong Il, the son of Kim Il Sung. U.S. leaders believe Kim Jong Il and the Korean People's Army remain a threat and continue to provide security in South Korea.

EPILOGUE

The men were evacuated to a M.A.S.H. unit about fifty kilometers from the 38th Parallel. The area separated the two warring factions of North and South Korea from one another, and it was far enough from the fighting that they could relax.

Rumors of the soldiers' acts of heroism quickly spread through the small mobile hospital. The stories filled everyone with feelings of inspiration. The men started to believe that the brutal war could be won with American know-how and determination.

But not everyone felt that way.

A lone figure sat in the quad between all the M.A.S.H. unit tents. He looked into the air as the medical helicopters roared off into the distance.

"This stinks," Corporal Soares said. He sat in his wheelchair, staring at the blue skies.

"Ah, you'll be up and playin' basketball again in no time," Richards said, strolling up behind him. On his face, there was a small bandage where the doctors had stitched up his cut.

"And DeLori?" asked Soares.

"It's too close to tell right now," said Donovan, walking with Reed.

"We're just lucky any of us got out of there alive," complained Soares. "That Lieutenant Polaski almost got us all killed."

"Actually, the LT was right," said Richards. He pulled a pair of mud-caked dog tags from his pocket and handed them to Corporal Soares.

Looking at him in shock, Soared growled. "Whose are these?" he asked.

"Polaski's," said the sergeant. "That armored patrol was actually out looking for us."

"Really?" asked Reed.

"Yeah," Richards said. "Seems the pilot's mayday got through. They would've rescued us in an hour."

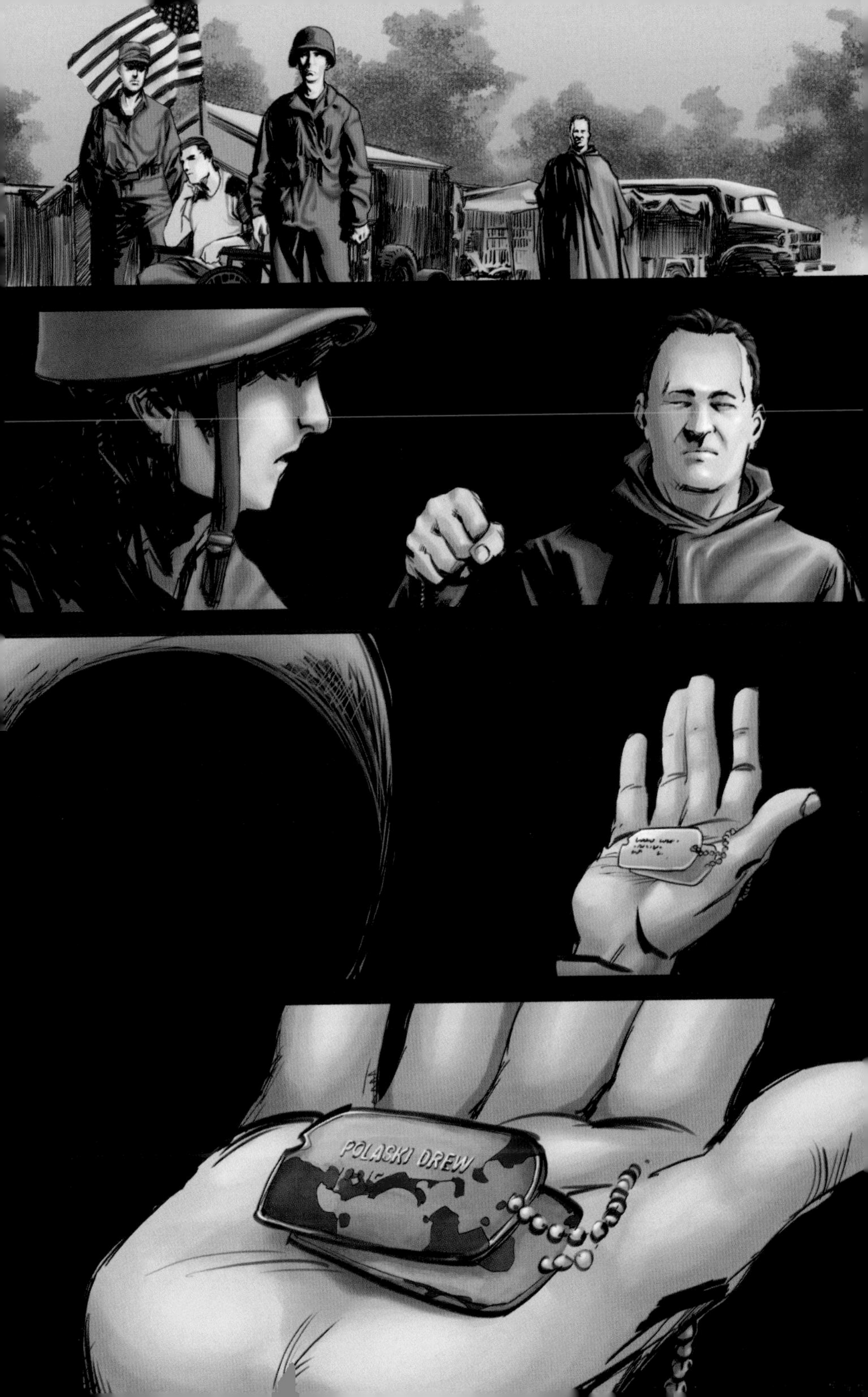
POLASKI DREW

"Problem with being in charge is having to make decisions that impact other people's lives," Richards said. "Polaski played it by the book, and he was right. They did come for us."

"But if we had stayed and waited, how many of us would have been alive by the time they'd gotten there?" Soares asked.

"Try not to judge him too harshly, Pete," Donovan said. He placed a hand on his friend's shoulder. "Polaski only did what he thought was right."

"And in this life, boys, that's all any of us can ever do," Richards said softly.

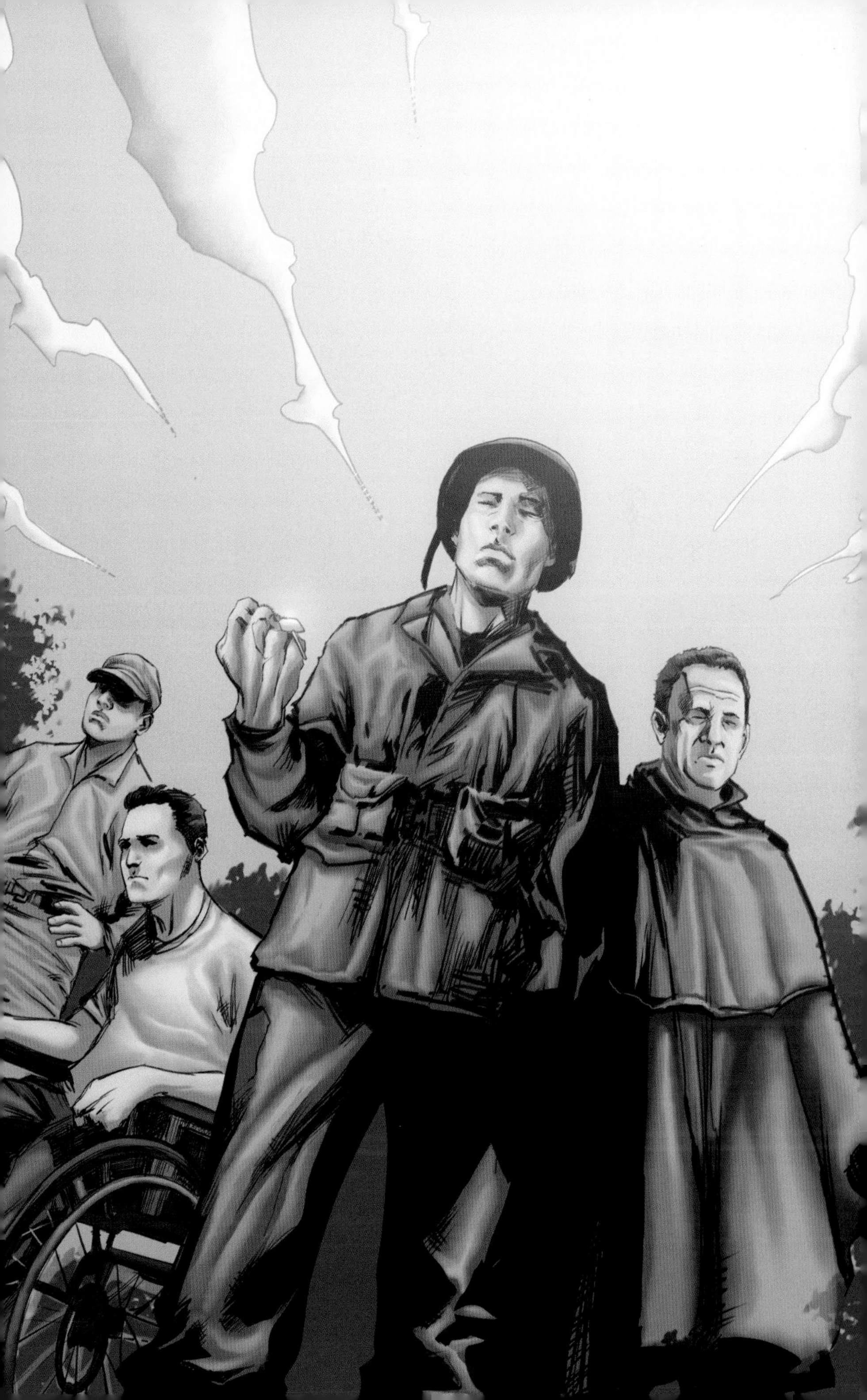

EXTRAS

ABOUT THE AUTHOR

M. ZACHARY SHERMAN is a veteran of the United States Marine Corps. He has written comics for Marvel, Radical, Image, and Dark Horse. His recent work includes *America's Army: The Graphic Novel, Earp: Saint for Sinners,* and the second book in the SOCOM: SEAL Team Seven trilogy.

AUTHOR Q&A

Q: Any relation to the Civil War Union General William Tecumseh Sherman?

A: Yes, indeed! I was one of the only members of my family lineage to not have some kind of active duty military participation – until I joined the U.S. Marines at age 28.

Q: Why did you decide to join the U.S. Marine Corps? How did the experience change you?

A: I had been working at the same job for a while when I thought I needed to start giving back. The biggest change for me was the ability to see something greater than myself; I got a real sense of the world going on outside of just my immediate, selfish surroundings. The Marines helped me to grow up a lot. They taught me the focus and discipline that helped get me where I am today.

Q: When did you decide to become a writer?

A: I've been writing all my life, but the first professional gig I ever had was a screenplay for Illya Salkind (*Superman* 1-3) back in 1995. But it was a secondary profession, with small assignments here and there, and it wasn't until around 2005 that I began to get serious.

Q: Has your military experience affected your writing?

A: Absolutely, especially the discipline I have obtained. Time management is key when working on projects, so you must be able to govern yourself. In regards to story, I've met and been with many different people, which enabled me to become a better storyteller through character.

Q: Describe your approach to the Bloodlines series. Did personal experiences in the military influence the stories?

A: Yes and no. I didn't have these types of experiences in the military, but the characters are based on real people I've encountered. And those scenarios are all real, just the characters we follow have been inserted into the time lines. I wanted the stories to fit into real history, real battles, but have characters we may not have heard of be the focus of those stories. I've tried to retell the truth of the battle with a small change in the players.

Q: Any future plans for the Bloodlines series?

A: There are so many battles through history that people don't know about. If they hadn't happened, the world would be a much different place! It's important to hear about these events. If we can learn from history, we can sidestep the mistakes we've made as we move forward.

Q: What's your favorite book? Favorite movie? Favorite video game?

A: My favorite book is *The Maltese Falcon* by Dashiell Hammett. I love a good mystery with hard-boiled detectives! As for movie, hands-down it's *Raiders of the Lost Ark*. It is a fantastic story of humanity winning out over evil and the characters are real people thrown into impossible odds. Lots of fun! As for games, there are way too many to mention, but I love sci-fi shooters and first-person games.

EXTRAS

ABOUT THE ILLUSTRATORS

Josef Cage is a Filipino artist based in Manila, Philippines. He currently works in advertising, creating storyboards for television commercials. He dreams of doing comics full-time someday. His most recent work is a comic book called *TRESE*.

Marlon Jay G. Ilagan is an artist, son, and brother. His fascination with the written word and storytelling led him into a career as a comic book colorist. He believes that stories are conversations between the creator and their audience, and he feels blessed to be a part of this discussion.

THE PROCESS

A CALL TO ACTION

WORLD WAR II

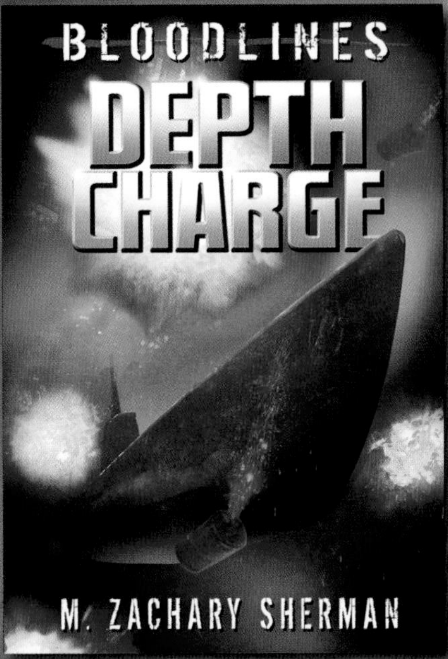
BLOODLINES
DEPTH CHARGE
M. ZACHARY SHERMAN

During World War II, British Intelligence discovers a German U-505 submarine anchored off the coast of Denmark. Stashed onboard are invaluable codebooks, keys to deciphering the enemy's communications. To secure the documents, a British commando and U.S. Army First Lieutenant Aaron Donovan must team up, sneak aboard the enemy submarine, and get off alive!

KOREAN WAR

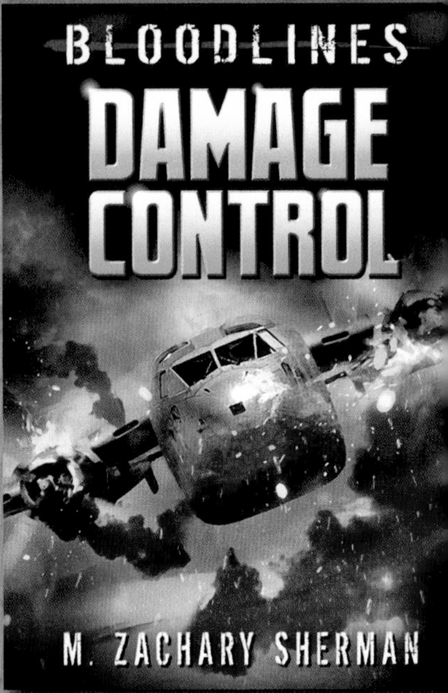
BLOODLINES
DAMAGE CONTROL
M. ZACHARY SHERMAN

During the Korean War, a U.S. Army cargo plane crashes behind enemy lines, and soldiers of the 249th Engineer Battalion are stranded. Facing a brutal environment and attacks by enemy forces, Private First Class Tony Donovan takes action! With spare parts and ingenuity, he plans to repair a vehicle from the wreckage and transport his comrades to safety.

VIETNAM WAR

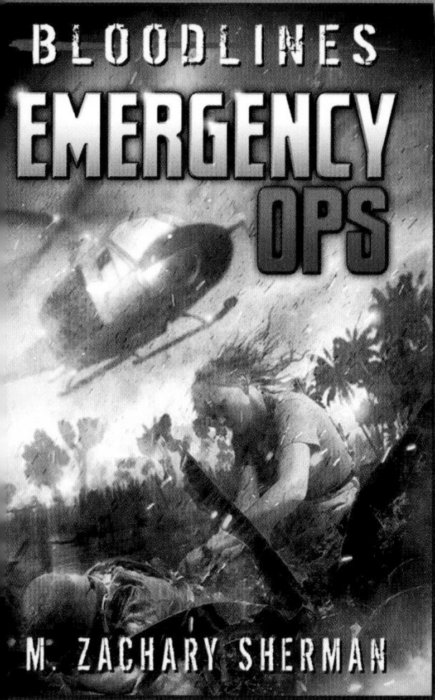

BLOODLINES
EMERGENCY OPS
M. ZACHARY SHERMAN

uring the Vietnam War, Captain nne Donovan of the U.S. Army urse Corps heads to the front lines. long with a small medical unit, ne'll provide aid to the soldiers at amburger Hill. But when the bloody attle intensifies, and Donovan's nief surgeon is critically wounded / sniper fire, this rookie nurse uickly becomes the leader of an nergency operation.

IRAQ WAR

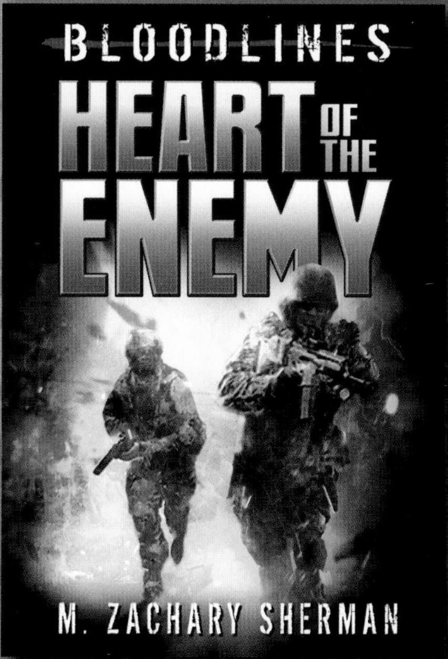

BLOODLINES
HEART OF THE ENEMY
M. ZACHARY SHERMAN

During the War in Iraq, Lieutenant Commander Lester Donovan of the U.S. Navy SEALs must capture a known terrorist near the border of Syria. It's a dangerous mission. Land mines and hostile combatants blanket the area, yet Donovan is undeterred. But when the mission goes awry, this gung-ho commander must learn to keep his cool, if he's going to keep his men alive.

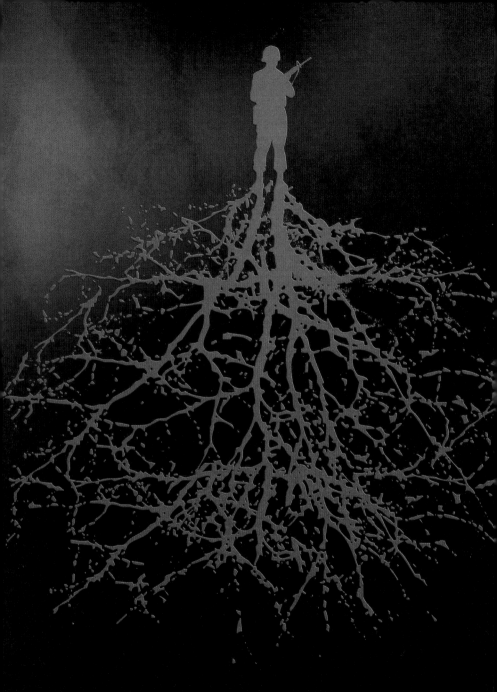

BLOODLINES

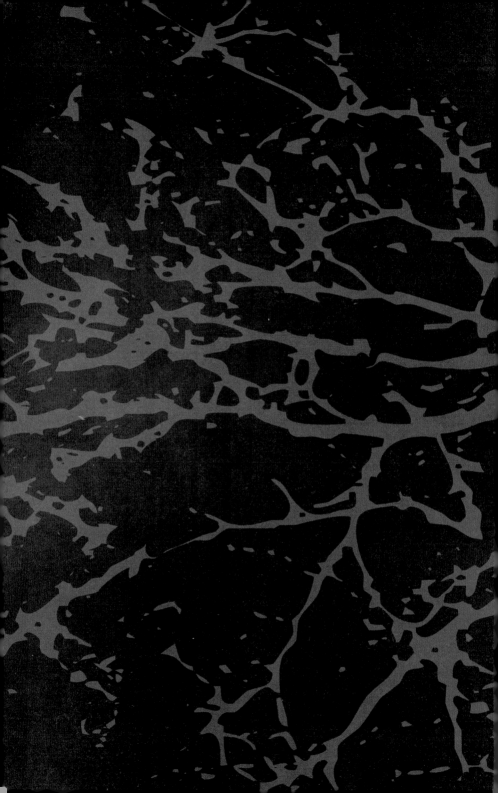

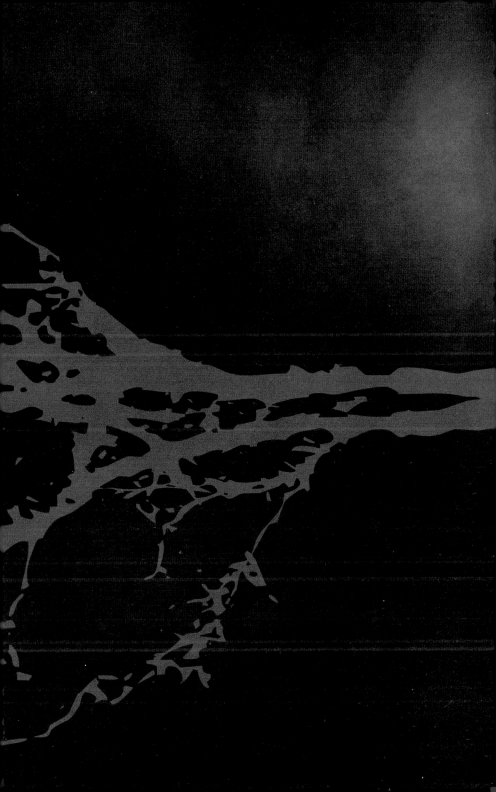